SUITE CASUALTY

CEECEE JAMES

For my Family

CONTENTS

BLURB

Maisie Swenson has seen a lot of strange things in her career as a hotel manager, so when Mr. Dayton insists there are ghosts in his suite, she handles it with her usual aplomb. And when he demands she visit his room to show her the items that have been moved, she suspects the two empty wine bottles and a half empty brandy bottle might be where the "ghosts" come from.

To reassure him, she posts a guard outside his room but in the morning, Mr. Dayton is found dead. With nothing removed from his suite, and no way in, rumors fly around that maybe he really was killed by ghosts after all. Or his own fear of them.

Maisie hopes the police will handle the investigation discreetly while she deals with an anonymous hotel critic who's threatening to tear down the Oceanside's reputation. But everything falls apart as Mr. Dayton's relatives start to show up—each one calling the other an imposter—demanding a letter Mr. Dayton was supposed to have on him. As they start to threaten each other, and then Maisie herself, she starts to suspect the spirits that killed Mr. Dayton are still contained in living bodies.

CHAPTER 1

*I*t wasn't every day that started with a slice of Texas sheet cake for breakfast. Mmm. I took a bite, juggling the plate in one hand while standing like a flamingo in the kitchen doorway, watching TV. My mother had left it tuned to that crazy crime station that she was addicted to, and the announcer was solemnly advising us, "There are no coincidences when it comes to murder."

I hummed again as the frosting's rich chocolatey-butterness melted in my mouth and turned back to the fridge to get out the milk.

A shuffling sound made me realize I wasn't alone. Momma had come into the kitchen from the other side, wearing a pink housecoat and worn slippers. Her strawberry-blonde hair recently had been "rinsed" by her favorite stylist, Genessa, and was springing out in fluffy curls. "Rinsing" is what Momma called getting her hair colored. She sniffed at the term 'dyed,' believing the word was entirely too uncouth.

"Louisa May Marigold Swenson. Just what do you think you're doing?" She stared at me over the tops of her glasses.

"Eating the most delectable thing on earth since God sent manna," I took another bite and mmmed again.

Momma blinked at my explanation. I could practically see her wheels spinning since I'd offered her so many directions to go with her response.

Finally, she settled on, "I hardly believe it's charitable to compare what the good Lord made to that lard-covered kaka. And heaven knows she used about a pound of it."

The "she" Momma was referring to was her old friend, Alice Bernsky, who had popped in for a visit the day before. Alice and Momma went way back to high school, and there had always been a friendly rivalry between the two them. So imagine Momma's displeasure when Alice showed up with a homemade cake whereas Momma had only prepared a snack of sweet tea and cookies. Alice had known she'd scored the win, and Momma was still salty about it.

I scraped up the last bit of frosting and licked the fork. It was so good. I would have been tempted to lick the plate if Momma hadn't been standing there. But, by the narrowing of her eyes, I realized I'd better do some fast back-tracking, or I'd never hear the end of it.

"Definitely not as good as yours, Momma. I bet she even used store-bought frosting. Probably used a boxed cake mixed too, all dolled up with an extra egg." I carried my plate to the sink and rinsed it.

She stared at me for a moment, suspicion gleaming from behind her wire-rimmed specs, before her ire settled down. She shuffled over to make a cup of coffee. "You better believe it. And I wouldn't doubt about the extra egg. That entire cake was much too heavy."

Crisis averted, I changed the subject. "So what do you have planned for today?"

She ignored my question and brought her mug to the table with the kind of quiet that always made me wary. I waited for a second to see if she'd volunteer anything.

Nope. Nothing.

I groaned. "All right, fess up. What's caught your eye on Pinterest this week?" I asked, sticking the plate in the dishwasher. Bingo, our Basset Hound, sniffed the door as I shut it and stared up at me with terribly sad eyes. I could tell he was disappointed that he didn't even get a crumb.

"Pinterest!" Momma gasped as if I'd just dared accuse her of bank robbery.

"Mmhmm," I answered.

She scowled at me. I held her stare with my hands on my hips and then, slowly, I drew my gaze up to the ceiling where a pink stain remained from her last Pinterest craft attempt.

She threw her hands up with a defeated sigh.

I was about to press her for an answer when my cell phone rang.

It was Sierra, one of the Oceanside hotel's receptionists.

"Ms. Swenson." The young woman's voice was low, indicating to me that not only was there a problem, the problem was more than likely to be standing straight in front of her. "Can you come to the front desk please?"

"I'm on my way," Professionalism slipped over me like a heavy wool coat. The Oceanside hotel was a five-star hotel, and I was the on-site manager. Time to gear up into rescue mode. I could feel it.

I clicked the phone off and turned to Momma. Desperation made me want to beg, so I purposely lightened my tone. "Please don't do anything crazy until I get back. I can't afford to keep redoing the apartment."

She waved her hand at me and muttered, "Pish posh."

I gave her a quick hug before running to find my heels I'd kicked off the night before. Before leaving the suite, I checked myself in front of the hall mirror for any stray cake crumbs and straightened my business jacket, then hurried for the hotel's foyer.

My heels clicked against the flooring as I walked. On my way, I eyed the oak wainscoting lining the hall. Everything must be perfect, from the polished wood surfaces to the lush Egyptian carpets.

The foyer was crowded with guests, and I could hear them mulling around as I approached. Crowning the hotel's entrance like a queen's scepter was a massive chandelier, with its hundreds of cut prisms throwing out tiny rainbows against the ceiling from the sun that peeked through the vaulted windows.

I walked over to the front desk. Sierra glanced up at my approach. The blonde receptionist wore a fitted business dress suit similar to my own. Her thin eyebrows pinched together in anxiousness.

Standing across from her was a slightly overweight gray-haired man. His hair was long, and he wore it slicked back in a pompadour across his scalp, presumably in an attempt to hide a balding patch. His arms waved about as he spoke.

Sierra nodded at his words, but he seemed to be frustrated by her reaction because he punctuated his thought with an emotionally wrought, shrill, "It's true, I'm telling you!"

I sidled up to the desk. His gaze jumped to me. "Ms. Swenson! You're just the person I've been looking for!"

I recognized him right away. He was Mr. Vincent Dayton, from the suite on the thirty-first floor. His lawyer had made the reservation for an early check-in, and Mr. Dayton arrived yesterday morning. He'd just returned from a business trip and would be leaving tomorrow.

His check-in had been a bit of a curiosity because of a few specific demands he'd made. For instance, his reservation was under a false name. That was quite common for our celebrities, as well as other guests who abided by the "what happens at the hotel stays at the hotel" rule, so it was something I normally didn't think too much about it. But he'd coupled it with a clear stipulation that no one was to enter his room, not room service nor the turndown crew. And the strangest of all was the instructions he'd given when he put a leather envelope into the hotel safe. He'd said that the item inside shouldn't be touched by anyone but him, and could only be released to his attorney in the unexpected event of his death.

I took a step back to avoid one of his waving arms. "Good

morning, Mr. Dayton," I said briskly to take control of the situation. "What can I do for you?"

He glanced around the foyer before leaning in close to me. I stifled my natural reaction to step away at the boozey odor that swam around him like a cloud of smog.

"Someone's been in my room," he hissed. "My clothing... it's been gone through. And I thought I saw—" He bit back the end of his sentence with a gulp.

I nodded firmly so that he understood I was taking his statement seriously. "I see. Let's go take care of that. Why don't you come into my office?" I suggested.

The wrinkles around his eyes deepened momentarily as if he were confused by my suggestion. Then, after my words had a moment to sink in, his face relaxed as if he were relieved.

"Yes. Thank you. That would be perfect." He gave another furtive glance around the foyer at the other guests milling about.

It was normal to see so much commotion. Our hotel was just off the beach, and near one of the biggest amusement parks in the country. At this time of day, most of the guests were either heading for breakfast or leaving for their planned excursions. Still, I could see the other guests' presence really bothered him.

"Right this way," I gestured to my office door behind the desk.

He followed me with his shoulders hunched in as though he were trying to hide.

I unlocked the door and went in, touching the armrest of one of the two guest chairs to welcome him to sit as I passed. Then I took my chair behind my desk.

"What's going on?" I asked, folding my hands, my face settling into a serious expression. "Who's been in your room?" Because of his explicit instructions, I knew it couldn't be any of my staff.

His head swiveled as he studied my office, his gaze jumping from picture frames to the bookcases. "Have you had this room debugged recently?"

A laugh almost escaped me at the absurd statement, but I managed to wrangle it back. I smiled calmly while my fingers went searching for a rubber band I normally kept by the keyboard. Finding it, I slipped it around my wrist and twirled it. Keeping my fingers moving was somehow a stress reliever for me.

"No, I can't say I have," I answered. "But no one has access to this office except who I allow."

"Oh, you think they can't get in?" His bloodshot eyes locked with mine. My breath caught at his intensity. "They go where they want. There's nothing you can hide from them."

I nodded, wondering if I was going to have to call security. Still, it was my job to diffuse these types of situations. "Who is 'them' exactly?"

He jammed his thumbnail into his mouth and bit viciously at it. "Them. Anyone they want to be."

I nodded again. "I see. Well, I'll check into that. But in the meantime, what can I do to help you feel more secure?"

His eyes darted to the wall safe. "Is my stuff still in there?"

I followed his gaze. "Of course. Unless you've removed it."

"Can you check?" His hands were shaking and he gripped the armrest.

I eased out a silent sigh. Best just to reassure him. "Yes. Of course, I can. Let me get Sierra. It takes both of our keys to open it."

"And you haven't done that?" His voice raised at the end of the question.

"No, Mr. Dayton. And once it's opened, you must sign the log book. We have several safeguards. No one has been in your safe deposit box here at the hotel."

He leaned back in his chair from where he'd been perched on

the edge. His eyelids fluttered closed. "I'm so tired, Ms. Swenson."

"I can see that. Would you like me to make an appointment with a massage therapist for you? We have an excellent one here at the hotel."

His eyes flew open, and I was startled to see how blue they were. "No. I want no one to go into the room. Remember? Including housekeeping. Understand?"

I nodded. "Of course. Whatever you want. All the staff knows your wishes."

"You're absolutely sure?"

"Yes, Mr. Dayton." I softened my voice. "Why don't you tell me what brought you down here this morning? You said someone had been in your room? Was there a particular reason why you thought this?"

He licked his lip and rubbed his hands together. I waited for a response. Finally, he gave me an uneasy smile. His teeth were yellow. "I must have been mistaken. It's been a long night. I'm still tired from my trip back from Madrid. Sometimes I get confused. I'm sorry to have bothered you." He rubbed his whiskered face and slowly rose to his feet.

I was taken a bit off guard at the sudden reversal of his

panicked attitude. I stood also and placed my hands at my back. My fingers spun the rubber band.

"That's absolutely no problem," I said. "It's what we're here for, to make your stay as comfortable as possible. If you have any other concerns, please don't hesitate to let any one of us know."

He walked to the door, barely lifting his feet, looking every bit sixty-plus years that I guessed he was, and then some.

"Thank you," he said and opened the door.

I breathed out in relief as he exited, feeling a little surprised that he was letting go so easily, given how worked up he'd been. But just before the door completely closed, it was shoved open again.

His head poked around the corner, eyebrows raised. "Do you know if this hotel is haunted?"

CHAPTER 2

I blinked hard at his question. Normally, I was able to hide my emotions, but his question threw me off guard.

"Not that I know of, Mr. Dayton. Is there a reason why you ask?"

His eyebrows lowered and his head drooped heavily. "Just something I thought I saw last night. Must have been a shadow." He sighed and shut the door.

At the latch's click, I slumped back down into my chair. *Okay, this guy needs to be watched.* He was definitely acting out of the realms of normal. I picked up the phone and dialed security.

"Mike here," one of my guards answered. His deep voice

brought quickly to mind the hulking guard. He worked the night shift and was built like a house, making Mike easily one of the female guests' favorite employee here at the hotel. And among the employees as well. Remembering how a group of housekeepers had giggled when he walked by made me realize I needed to keep a sharp eye on him.

"Good morning, Mike. Do you remember our guest up in suite 360? His name is Mr. Dayton. Came in on Monday."

It was part of the job for the guards to know who was checked in at the hotel, especially in the expensive suites. So, each morning, security had a meeting to go over the guest list.

"360. Okay, got it," he said. I presumed he was looking at his list on the tablet.

"He came down this morning saying that someone had been in his room. He was quite agitated."

"The room no one's supposed to enter," Mike clarified.

"Yes. We had a talk in my office, and strangely, he recanted his story. He seems unpredictable, and I'd like to keep an eye on him. So please let the guard know who's taking over your shift."

"You got it. Sent the alert out now."

"Thanks, Mike. Also, I'd like to be informed if and when Mr. Dayton leaves the hotel."

He agreed, and we hung up.

I pushed back from the desk and twisted the rubber band as I replayed the conversation with Mr. Dayton. My mind zeroed in on his shaking hands and paranoia. It could be nothing. He could be affected by jet lag, or some use of medication, prescribed or otherwise.

But something about his actions nagged at my intuition. And if there was one thing I'd learned during my thirty-five years on this planet, it was to pay attention to that small inner voice.

Well, Mike and the rest of security were aware of the issue, now.

My phone vibrated with a text, interrupting my thoughts. It was from Mr. Phillips, the hotel's owner. I hit the button to read, —**Call me.**

I dialed immediately.

"Ms. Swenson," Mr. Phillips' deep, somewhat pompous voice cut to the chase. "I've heard a little rumor that there will be a hotel critic posturing as one of our guests sometime in the next couple days. I don't need to tell you that it's imperative that everything runs perfectly. We want to keep our five-star rating."

My stomach dropped at the word *critic*. Having experienced

a few as a manager, I knew it wouldn't be hard to tell who he or she was. They were the worst and set every employee on edge.

"Yes, sir. You've got it, sir. I'll tell the staff to be on their toes," I answered.

His response was gruff. "I'm counting on you, Maisie. If anything were to happen to our rating, there is a possibility there will be cutbacks in the staff."

"No worries, sir. We've got this." My voice was confident, but my insides quaked.

He hung up. I wasn't sure he even heard my reply. Sighing, I flipped on the computer and sent the heads of my staff a message to gather for an emergency meeting in an hour.

A red alert for an email message blinked at me. I opened it to see it was from Julie Jenkins, the head of our housekeeping, with a complaint about some coffee pot issue. There was another from Sierra asking if she should put suite 359 back into rotation. Apparently, the guest who'd reserved it for three days hadn't shown up. I rubbed my cheek and then set up an appointment to talk with Julie straight after the meeting, and then advised Sierra to give the guest until three o'clock today.

It had already been a busy morning with just those few fires to put out. But nothing had happened that was too out of the ordinary.

Or so I thought.

———

An hour later, the heads of staff had gathered in the meeting hall, along with any other employees who could attend.

I walked to the front and put on my best cheerleader/confident leader smile. "Okay, everyone. I'm setting you all on alert. Mr. Phillips heard through the grapevine that we're about to have an extra special guest."

The room started buzzing with talk. I spotted a couple of the new girls in the back whispering with huge grins on their faces. I'm sure they were picturing 'extra special' as a celebrity.

But a senior worker standing next to them shook her head. Most of the employees had been here long enough to know exactly what 'extra special' meant.

"That's right." I clasped my hands before me. "A hotel critic." Groans sounded off around the room. I pushed through them. "So, as we know all too well, extra special means extra attention, extra service, and extra work. You guys can handle this with your eyes closed, but this is just a reminder to please pay attention to every detail over the next few days. After all, we pride ourselves on our rating, right? We know we're worth it, and we will continue to prove it. Any questions?"

There were a few raised hands. I quickly fielded through them and then dismissed the group with a little more cheerleading.

As everyone filtered out of the room, I waved at Julie to come over to talk with me. The little woman walked up, her lips pressed together into two grim lines. She tried to smile, but the smile never reached her eyes.

Normally, this housekeeper was an abundant source of joyous energy that I'd previously only witnessed in a Disney cartoon, and I was concerned.

"You okay?" I asked.

Julie shrugged.

Right. Super convincing. "What's going on? Anything I can do to help?"

"Ms. Swenson, we're having a problem with the bed sheets. They're getting ruined, and we're losing them left and right. Also, there must be a popular new video going around online about hotel hacks."

"Disappearing bed sheets? Hotel hacks? What do you mean?"

"I'm telling you, in the last two days, I've had to scrub out over twenty-three coffee pots. Guests are using them to make ramen noodles. Eggs even!" She sighed and groaned out, "They've even been using the irons to cook bacon. You have no idea the amount of grease I've seen." Her mouth slanted pitifully.

My eyebrows rose. I shouldn't be surprised after everything I'd seen, but I was. "You're kidding me."

"No! I wish I was. If these people want a kitchen, they should rent a room with a kitchen." She crossed her arms.

I rubbed my temples as imagined complaints of freshly ironed, bacon-scented clothes ping-ponged in my head. And that was nothing compared to what I'd hear if the guest's coffee tasted like ramen noodles. Heaven forbid if you messed with a person's morning coffee.

Better not mess with mine.

Well, it was a good excuse for me to push for Mr. Phillips to switch the hotel over to those single serve coffee pod machines. Not only would it end misuse of the decanters, but those machines made a pretty good cup of coffee.

But trying to modernize the hotel was always a slow business. I could practically see dollar signs ringing in Mr. Phillips' pupils whenever I brought up improvements, as he added up the cost.

I reassured Julie that I'd take care of it, and she left the conference room. Rubbing my neck, I headed back to my office, where I started my daily tasks of checking on the guest requests, revamping work schedules for my hotel staff, and itemizing hotel merchandise that needed to be ordered. I ordered more bed sheets and then started drafting a letter to Mr. Phillips concerning the coffee pots.

It was after two, and I'd just thought about maybe stopping to get a late lunch when my phone buzzed. It was from Sierra and it simply said—**Code Blue.**

CHAPTER 3

*C*ode Blue already? That meant the hotel critic was at the front desk checking in earlier than normal. But guests could request that with their reservation. I hurried from my office and smoothed down my skirt, trying to appear casual as I glanced down the guests in line waiting.

Ah. It must be that woman standing in front of Clarissa. Thin, in her upper forties, the woman had a nose so sharp it looked like the edge of a sheer mountain crag. The woman's hair was cut in an old pageboy style with thick bangs, and an oversize baby-pink colored leather purse sat on the counter next to her. She wore sunglasses as she addressed Clarissa.

I never understood why people wore sunglasses indoors.

"Exactly where is my room?" the woman asked, her voice

loud and demanding. "It's not above the pool, is it? Your website didn't make that clear."

"The north tower does not overlook the pool," Clarissa reassured with a sweet smile.

"Well, I hope the view isn't of the parking lot. Tell me, is it of the parking lot?"

Clarissa glanced down at the screen. "I do believe it's at the far end of our parking lot. It also happens to give a glimpse of the Starke Springs park."

"No, I absolutely can't abide that. Can't you change the room? I abhor parking lots."

Clarissa's fingers flew over the keyboard with mad tapping. After a second, she said with a sympathetic tone, "I'm sorry. I don't think we have a room comparable to what you've reserved. I'm afraid the hotel is booked at the moment, but if there are any cancellations—"

"Honestly, you call yourselves a five-star hotel?" The woman's voice rose.

I sailed in behind the desk to stand near Clarissa for support. The receptionist looked at me with a worried frown. "Ms. Swenson, do you think you might be able to do something here?"

With a firm smile both at Clarissa and the woman, I asked, "How can I help?"

The woman looked at me with pursed lips. She took in my business attire and realized who I was. Her spine stiffened with validation.

Clarissa introduced us. "This is Mrs. Devin Richardson, and..."

Mrs. Richardson interrupted her. "I'm trying to get a room that doesn't overlook the parking lot, but it appears they've all been taken. However, your website doesn't state the views of the room when I reserved it."

Our website did show rooms with a view, which were clearly laid out in the preference section of choices. Of course, those rooms came at a premium price as well.

"Let's see what we have." I sent her another smile and moved the keyboard slightly in my direction. I knew Clarissa had already done this, but sometimes the guests didn't believe the receptionist and made me give them the same news. Clarissa took a step back to allow me a bit of room.

Sure enough, after typing for a few moments, I could only confirm what Clarissa had already said. The only remaining rooms were on the side of the hotel that the critic was trying to get away from.

Mrs. Richardson tapped a manicured nail against the counter and leaned back, clearly growing impatient. I caught a glimpse of a hotel review card poking from the inside pocket of her jacket and quickly made up my mind. I scrolled through the suites. Room 359 that Sierra had asked about earlier still showed up as vacant. I bit my lip trying to decide.

The taps on the counter increased.

I smiled at her. "Good news. We can upgrade you to suite 359, on the thirty-first floor. It overlooks the state park and even gives you a peek-a-boo glimpse of the ocean."

"Peek-a-boo." The woman sniffed and opened her purse. Out came a small notebook where she jotted something with a silver pen. She put it away and smiled back. "That sounds fine."

I moved to allow Clarissa control of the keyboard. The receptionist typed in the reservation and then slid over the room key.

"I hope you enjoy your stay," I said. "If you need anything else, please let me know. I'm here twenty-four hours a day."

"I'll be ringing you if I have any problems, have no doubt about that." Mrs. Richardson exited the line and walked to the elevator. Her bag, a small one, was already in the hands of one of our bellhops.

I pulled the front of my shirt away. That woman had me sweating already.

THE REST of the day passed by easily enough, ending with a quiet night back in my suite. In fact, I'd just settled into my bed with my newest book—a mystery I'd treated myself to for my birthday—when I got another phone call. I rolled over and grabbed it from the nightstand. It was Lisa, our night clerk.

"Ms. Swenson? Sorry to disturb you. Can you please call Mr. Dayton? He's insisting on speaking to you personally. He sounded quite perturbed."

"Of course, Lisa. Thanks for letting me know." I hung up and dialed his room number. What was going on with this man? Was he having delusions again? I glanced at the clock—nine p.m.—and realized I hadn't heard from any of the guards, which meant Mr. Dayton most likely hadn't left his room all day.

The phone rang and rang.

No answer.

What in the world? I glanced at my closet. *I'm going to have to get dressed and run up there, aren't I?*

The phone was answered with a gasp. "Hello?"

"Mr. Dayton?"

"Yes." His voice quavered.

"Hi, there. My receptionist informed me that you wanted a call. Is everything okay?"

There was a long pause on the other end. What on earth was going on?

"I wouldn't say okay," he finally said.

Something was very wrong. I jumped out of bed and grabbed a pair of pants. "I'll be right up. Do you need me to call an ambulance?"

"No!" He yelled, his fear-stricken voice cutting through the receiver like a blade. "No. Don't call anyone. I'm ... okay. But please come up."

I swallowed and slipped on my shoes. The phone felt tacky in my sweating palm. "I'm on my way. Is there anything you need?"

"No. Just you." The phone cut off.

Well, there was no way it was going to be "just me" going up there. My spider sense was tingling. Something was going on. I called security.

Mike answered again. He'd already been home all day and was starting a new night shift.

"Hey, can you meet me at the elevator? I need to go up to room 360."

"Still problems with that Dayton guy? Security said he was quiet all day. What's going on?"

"I just spoke with him on the phone and he sounded really off. It's probably nothing but I want to be prepared."

"Yeah, you got it. I'll meet you at the elevator."

We hung up, and I finished dressing. I slipped the phone into my pocket and a lanyard that held the all room pass-key over my head. Then, quietly I shut the bedroom door and tip-toed down the hall, hoping not to disturb Momma. She had ears like a bat.

The floor squeaked, and I froze.

"Maisie?" Momma called from her room. Her voice was a tinge higher with concern. "What's going on, darlin'?"

"Nothing, Momma. Just going to help one of the guests who needs some assistance."

"At this time of night?"

I smiled. Momma always went to bed at eight-thirty on account of her needing beauty sleep. I peeked into Momma's bedroom.

Bingo was on the bed, the dog's snout inches from Momma's

face. The blankets were tucked around the Basset Hound, and one of Bingo's crocodile paws rested on the pillow. He was snoring, lip flaps quivering.

There was a time when I used to nag at Momma for letting the dog on the bed because of the dangers to Bingo's spine. But Momma had shot that argument down with a Pinterest craft; a set of stairs made out of an old crate so the dog could climb up and down safely.

She stared at me now with dark beady eyes. "Is it a man or a woman?"

"What?"

"The guest that wants you to go tromping up there at this time of night. Man or woman?"

"It's a man."

"Well, you be careful, now. He might have been tipping back a few and decide he wants a certain kind of company." She raised a nonexistent eyebrow. With her makeup scrubbed off, her eyebrows went with it.

"Momma, I'm thirty-five. Trust me, I'm more than capable of taking care of myself."

She harrumphed and flopped over. "You may think you're so high and mighty, but you're my baby and I'll always worry."

I smiled. "Love you too, Momma."

"You just check in with me when you get back. I won't get a wink of beauty sleep while you're gone. And I sure need it because tomorrow is game night and Mr. Carmichael will be there. And so will Tawny Myers. That woman's been setting her eyes on him, I swear. I noticed she's changed her hair color to an awful shade of red. And positively bathing in White Musk." She fretted at the sheet.

"Momma, you don't have a thing to worry about. Tawny has nothing on you. Get some sleep. I'll be back in a little while. And as for the hotel guest, I'm bringing Mike up to the room for added security." The inward jokester sparked then and I couldn't resist adding, "But maybe you *should* think about buying some White Musk."

Momma rolled back over with an indignant, "Louisa Mae Marigold Swenson!" Bingo opened one eye at being disturbed.

I laughed. "I'm just kidding. You're beautiful, and you know it."

She relaxed back on the pillow. "And you're a petal off the ol' flower."

I smiled as I shut her door. That woman cracked me up. I was lucky to have her as my mom.

It was still noisy in the foyer as families returned for the night and couples left to take in the nightlife. Mike stood outside the elevator, his big shoulders back. He caught the eye and nodded at a young lady. She returned his smile and sauntered over to him.

Inwardly, I groaned. I really didn't want to catch him flirting with one of our guests. That was something Mr. Phillips was a stickler about, and with the owner's threats about letting the staff go, I wasn't taking any chances. I hurried over, my heels clacking loudly.

Mike glanced in my direction and the easy smile fell off his face as it morphed into a professional expression.

The young lady was confused until she turned and saw me. "So, I'll talk to you later, Mike." She giggled.

"Yes, Miss Clark," he said in a clipped tone.

She strolled away, hips swaying.

"Well, then, Mike," I said, one eyebrow raised.

He flushed guiltily and cleared his throat. "Ms. Swenson," he said.

"What's Mr. Phillips' rule about fraternizing with the guests?" I pushed the elevator button.

"Absolutely not, under any circumstances."

I didn't respond, letting my silence do the talking for me.

"She, uh, she needed help getting a taxi and, uh…"

"Under no circumstances," I echoed back to him.

"Yes, ma'am," he said, his head drooping.

The doors opened with a ding, and we entered. I punched in the numbers for the thirty-first floor and glanced at Mike again. He gave me a cheesy grin and a shrug, to which I rolled my eyes.

CHAPTER 4

The elevator door clunked just before it opened, making my eyebrows shoot up. Mike and I headed out. The plush carpet stifled our footfalls. The air was thick with the scent of carpet freshener that the staff used every other day.

"Now, I want you to remain calm. Mr. Dayton might be having another episode," I warned.

Mike's jaw clenched as he seemed to prepare himself for what may lay ahead. We stopped outside room 360, and I firmly knocked.

No answer. I glanced at Mike and rapped hard on the door again. Mike shifted next to me as my hand automatically went to the lanyard around my neck. Was I going to have to unlock the door?

The door opened a crack. The heavy brass ball clanged as it slid to the end of the metal hasp.

"Mr. Dayton? It's me, Ms. Swenson."

A blue eye appeared at the door, surrounded by a mop of gray hair. Mr. Dayton sucked in his breath when he caught sight of Mike.

"No, he's fine," I hurriedly reassured the guest. "This is Mike, and he's hotel security. I wanted to bring him based on your earlier concerns."

Mr. Dayton licked his bottom lip and then the door shut. I stood there, unsure of what was going to happen next. Then a clicking sounded, and the door swung open. Mr. Dayton stepped back to let us in. He had on dark blue sweatpants and a wrinkled t-shirt. His rumpled appearance seemed to point to him just waking up.

"Someone was in here," he whispered hoarsely.

His tone spooked me slightly. I glanced around. The suite was dark with the only a soft glow coming from a nightlight in the closet alcove and the light spilling in from the hallway.

"In here?" I repeated.

"Yes. While I was sleeping."

"Was your door locked?" I asked. Mike turned the handle to check if it was working properly. But I knew the answer had to be yes. The suite doors all had an automatic secondary lock that kicked in when the door was shut.

Mr. Dayton ignored my question. "Someone touched my face."

His eyes were wild and crazy. I was unnerved, not sure if it was more from his words or his appearance. "Did you see the person?"

"It woke me up."

"What do you mean by *it*? The touch? Could it have been a dream?" I'd had things happen in dreams that I could have sworn were real.

"It." Dayton moved with zombie-like jerkiness toward the bed. "It touched me while I was sleeping and then disappeared. Just like a spirit."

A shiver ran down my back. "Do you mind if we turn on a light?" I asked. "We need to check around."

The light from the hall glinted on sweat on Dayton's pale face. His tongue darted out again, wetting his lip. Finally, he nodded—just one brief bob. Relieved, I reached for the switch and flipped it on.

He squinted as his hand flew up to block it as if the single bulb from the lamp were a thousand watts. On his nightstand, I saw two opened wine bottles. I watched his reaction closely, trying to decide if it was alcohol or drugs that was fueling his reactions.

"Sir? Are you okay?" Mike asked as if suspecting the same thing.

"Am I okay? How can I possibly be okay?" Mr. Dayton snarled at the security guard. "Something woke me from sound sleep by touching my face." He shivered and a hand scrubbed at his cheek, dark with stubble. "Can you even imagine that, Ms. Swenson? A cold hand reaching out—" Here he lifted his hand in my direction, his eyes locked on mine. "Touching your cheek. Such an intimate thing, the stroke of a person's skin against another. And the touch of the face the most intimate of all." His gaze snapped back to Mike's. "But when I opened my eyes, he was gone."

I swallowed. "Is it possible it was a nightmare?"

"A nightmare?" Dayton repeated it back like I was crazy. "Some vain imagination about being woken by another being? And what about that? Did I imagine that as well?" He pointed an accusing finger at a glass on the table, half full of an amber liquid.

Oh boy. "What's going on with the glass?" I asked.

"Are you bloody stupid?"

I felt my dander rankle at his words. "Excuse me?" I asked coldly.

"Just look! Look at that glass!"

I walked over and saw one of our courtesy bottles opened and empty.

"Yes?" I asked.

"That's brandy. I never drink it and certainly didn't open the bottle. Someone came in here and opened that. Someone drank half of it while they watched me sleep." He twisted around to stare at his bed and shivered again. "And then they touched me."

Definitely drunk. Or something else. "Well, Mr. Dayton. How about if Mike takes a quick look around your suite to make sure it's secure? You didn't hear anyone leave after you woke?"

"Leave?" His brow wrinkled, now making him look less deranged and more like a confused old man. "No. No one left." He sank to the bed. "I keep trying to tell you. I opened my eyes, and they were gone. My heart was hammering so much, I could barely find the phone."

"How is your heart feeling now?" I asked.

35

"My heart? It feels like I've been scared nearly to death by an intruder." His eyes widened. "Tell me the truth. This room is haunted, isn't it? Something terrible has happened here. I can feel it. Evil. Death."

I shook my head. "No, sir. Nothing like that has happened. Would you like me to call you an ambulance? Just to be on the safe side. How about your lawyer?"

He glanced at me and then turned his face sadly. "Everyone's betrayed me. Even you don't believe me."

"Sir, I think there are a lot of things that can happen while we're dreaming that seem so real. But I do believe that something happened to upset you. Mike," I gestured to the security guard to get him to investigate.

Mike jumped from his place by the door and began a careful search of the suite. He moved the drapes, walked into the large closet, and examined the bathroom. He came back out and walked to the sliding door. We watched him examine the lock to make sure it was engaged before unlocking it and walking out onto the deck. Mike's lips were pressed together when he came back inside. Carefully, he locked the door and then glanced at me, giving me the slightest shake of his head.

"So, it appears your suite is secure." I tried to make my tone sound light-hearted. "Now, about that ambulance."

Dayton shook his head wearily. "No ambulance."

I nodded. "All right. If you're sure. You will be safe tonight. I think it's possible that it may have been a realistic nightmare brought on by jet-lag. I've seen it happen before." I hadn't, but I wanted to reassure him.

"And that?" He pointed to the glass.

I thought the only option was that he opened it himself and didn't remember. After all, the two opened wine bottles attested to him being quite inebriated. Still, it wasn't proper to accuse the guests of drinking too much.

"I'm not sure about that," I said. "But I have a feeling that in the morning there will be a simple explanation."

"I don't like brandy," he reiterated again, his lips pushed forward in a pout.

"I understand. I don't care for it either. Perhaps you may have even had an episode of sleepwalking?"

"And sleep-drinking?" he asked sarcastically as if what I suggested was ridiculous. So much more ridiculous than having us run up here in search of an intruder who magically disappeared?

"I think this place is haunted," he said. " And I think you're hiding something."

His line of reasoning was absurd. I decided to humor him like I would a child. "This place is too new to be haunted. You'd find those places down closer to the center of town. There are a few stories I've heard...."

"It's nice to see you're taking this so seriously." His frustration flared.

My words fell flat in my throat. I swallowed as if I could erase them and then tried again. "Mr. Dayton, if anything else happens tonight, anything at all, please feel free to call me."

"You're leaving?" His eyes darted between me and Mike. He reached out and grabbed my arm. I frowned at his grip, pinching and desperate.

"Please don't leave me. Someone was in here, I tell you. Please!" Dayton's sweaty face turned toward Mike. "You believe me, don't you?" He smiled and nodded in eagerness to draw an agreement from the other man.

Mike's face was stoic. *Nod, Mike. Nod.* I silently begged. I was afraid Dayton was about to have a real break down.

"I have an idea," I said. "What if I have Mike patrol this floor? He'll guard your room and keep an eye on things. Would that make you feel safer, Mr. Dayton?"

The expression on Dayton's face was palpable with relief. Mike didn't appear nearly as pleased.

"That...that would be wonderful." The guest's trembling hand fell away from my arm. "Thank you."

"Absolutely. Now try to get some rest. We're not going to let anything happen to you." I walked to the door, again noting the disarray of the room. Dayton followed me out into the hallway. He stared down at the elevator as if to reassure himself that the hall was empty.

"You keep telling me to get some sleep," he mumbled. "But I think that's quite impossible between alcoholic ghosts and partiers upstairs."

I ignored the ghost comment. "Partiers? Have you heard a lot of noise from upstairs?"

He nodded, his bloodshot eyes half-closed.

"I'll take care of that, Mr. Dayton. Mike will be right outside, so if you hear anything, anything at all, just give a holler and we'll figure it out. Okay?"

He nodded again, his shoulders slumped forward in resignation. I felt terrible that he seemed to think I didn't believe him. But, I didn't, did I? After all, what he was saying was crazy.

I left Dayton locking his door. Mike followed me a few steps down the hall. I could tell the guard was unhappy with the way his boots shuffled a little heavier than usual. But, hey, I was the boss. It was my job to make sure things at the Oceanside Hotel ran smoothly and the guests were taken care of.

"Ms. Swenson," he hesitated. "While I was searching the suite, I found something the cleaning staff left."

"What? Where?"

"When I was checking out the bathroom area. It was in the closet." He pulled it out of his pocket. It was green, and I recognized it as a piece of one of the rubber gloves that housekeeping used when they cleaned.

"Okay, thanks," I said, reaching my hand to take it to throw out. He passed it over, and I shoved it into my business jacket pocket.

Room 359's door was open to the safety chain and Mrs. Richardson peeked through the crack.

"Everything okay?" I asked.

She eyed me for a moment and slammed the door shut.

Okay, then. I sighed and continued to the elevator. Before I could push the button, the door opened, and a group of tipsy young adults danced and twirled past me as they exited.

"Want to come party?" one young woman asked.

I couldn't help a smile, knowing I looked like a school teacher at my age and in my outfit. Yet I was still flattered they asked.

I shook my head, hoping they wouldn't disturb Dayton as well. "You guys have fun."

The woman didn't look disappointed at my refusal and continued to sing as she pirouetted away. My eyebrows lowered as I watched them enter their suite, and I wondered if I'd be hearing from the front desk about them later.

I got onto the elevator and hit the button. The elevator jerked as it started its descent, giving me a tiny jolt of adrenaline. No matter how many times I rode it, I never liked being in it.

I was tired and ready for my bed. I hoped the rest of the evening would be quiet. I headed to my suite where the competing snores of Bingo and Momma serenaded me as I walked through the door.

THE NEXT MORNING was business as usual. As I headed to my office, I dialed Mike to see how everything went.

"Good morning, Mike. How was the evening?"

"Everything quiet out here, Ms. Swenson. You mind if I take off? My shift's over."

"Have you heard from Mr. Dayton?"

"I heard some movement in his suite earlier, but no sign of him yet today."

"Okay. Knock on his door and let him know you're leaving. If there's a problem, let me know. And thank you. I appreciate the job well done."

"You got it. See you tonight."

I hung up with a smile. For the next twenty minutes, I toured the hotel, making sure everything was going smoothly. My employees were amazing, and I was a lucky boss. Even with the critic here, I wasn't too worried. Our customer service was number one. I was especially proud of our attached restaurant that offered a full custom breakfast with five-star chefs. And the upper suites were pools of luxury.

I stood outside one of our gyms that was better equipped than most of the name-brand sport's clubs and breathed with satisfaction. To be honest, I kind of enjoyed the challenge that having a critic in residence brought us. I had full confidence we were going to knock the socks off of the reviewer. Even with her vinegar-soaked personality.

It turns out, it only takes one monkey wrench to ruin the best-laid plans. And as I turned at the sound of pounding feet, I feared that monkey wrench was fast approaching in the form of Mike as he ran toward the gym.

Something told me I wasn't going to like what he was about to say.

"What's going on? Is Mr. Dayton okay?" I asked as my every nerve readied to spring into action.

"What?" Mike panted, his face flushed red. "Oh, yeah. I knocked on his door and he opened it to tell me that he was almost done packing. He should be checking out soon."

My mouth dropped open. Everything was fine. Mike had actually even seen him. I wanted to strangle the security guard for scaring me. "Why on earth did you run down here like it was an emergency?"

"Oh, geez." He glanced through the window at the guests in the weight room. "Uh, I wanted to personally tell you so you wouldn't worry."

I frowned as I studied him. He was lying to me. "How did you know where to find me?"

He smiled, his big meat-hands opening up as he shrugged. I watched him for a second longer and then held up a warning finger, "Be good, Mike."

"Of course." He chuckled. "Aren't I always? Anyway, since I let you know, I guess I'll be taking off."

"All right. Have a good night's sleep," I said as I walked past him, nearly bumping into Courtney, another part of our nighttime concierge service staff. She'd been racing out of the gym's doorway. I raised an eyebrow at the young woman, who looked flustered to see me.

"Hi, Ms. Swenson." she stammered.

"Hi, yourself. Are you heading home, now?" I asked.

"Yeah. Hi, Mike," Courtney glanced at Mike. Every speck of her makeup appeared touched up and fresh.

"Oh, hey, Courtney. I guess I'll see you tomorrow," Mike responded lamely.

I eyed them both. These kids, I swear. Staff dating was another thing against Mr. Phillip's rules.

Mike caught my look and rubbed the back of his neck before grinning cheekily at me.

Shaking my head, I walked away, off to my office to deal with my morning chores.

"Oh, Ms. Swenson!" A voice called.

I turned back around to see a woman who reminded me of a retired teacher. She had a towel wrapped over a swimsuit, and her hair was slicked back. Coupled with the fact that her skin was flushed and sweaty, I figured she was probably returning from one of the saunas.

"Good morning." I smiled. "How are you? Anything I can do to help you?"

"Oh, I'm great! This place is amazing. I just had to thank you for the fresh juice and ham croissant sent to my room this morning."

The hotel offered a simple complimentary breakfast with room service. "I'm so glad you liked it."

"And the bouquet of daisies! Such a lovely touch."

"It's our pleasure. What was your name?"

"Oh, I'm Jennifer. Jennifer Parkins. I'm just here for a little vacation. I figured even single people like going to theme parks, right?"

"Absolutely. You know it's called one of the greatest places on earth for a reason, and thousands of single people visit it every year. Me included. I hope you enjoy yourself, and if there is anything you need, anything at all, please don't hesitate to let one of the staff know."

"You bet. I just got out of Zumba, and then the sauna. Now I'm off to the pool."

"Sounds fun!" I waved goodbye and headed for my office. It was nice to see a guest so happy. Sometimes I really loved my job.

By four o'clock that afternoon, the rush of people had dropped to a trickle. It was the quiet hour right before the avalanche of room service requests and people leaving for dinner. I was just getting ready to grab my own dinner when Clarissa knocked on my office door.

"Ms. Swenson, the guest in room 360 still hasn't vacated yet."

I groaned. Mr. Dayton. "Have you sent someone up there to check on him?"

"Yes. There was a note in the computer. Apparently last night he requested a late checkout, so the night staff gave him until two today. At two-thirty, I rang the room and then sent the bellhop up to knock. There was no answer, but before I could deal with that, another call came in with a cleanup issue on the elevator." Clarissa wrinkled her nose. "A food poisoning incident. Projectile vomit everywhere."

Heaven help me. "Was the elevator sufficiently cleaned and disinfected?"

"Yes, it's been thoroughly cleaned. But I forgot about room 360 until now. I wanted to let you know."

I nodded. "Let's get someone up there now. Have you tried again?"

"I just rang the room before coming in here. There was no answer."

I closed my eyes and pressed my fingers against my temple. This was not good news. With a sigh, I called for security.

Steve answered this time. An older, burly man, Steve had been at the hotel longer than nearly every other employee.

"Steve, I need an escort up to room 360. Most likely there is a medical emergency. Can you meet me there?"

"Absolutely, Ms. Swenson."

Within five minutes, both Steve and I were both standing outside of Mr. Dayton's room. I rapped hard on the door before pulling out my pass-key. The door opened to the security lock. Steve removed an emergency tool from his belt and started to work on it.

The door to the next suite opened and Mrs. Richardson stuck her head out.

"What's all the racket?" she asked. Her pixie cut was haloed with a black velvet headband. She wore readers and stared at me over the tops of them. In her hand was a paperback.

I smiled. "Just clearing a room. That headband looks lovely," I added with a smile.

Her face took an oddly nostalgic expression as her eyes softened. She touched it with one finger. "This old thing was from my Juilliard School days."

"Did you dance?" I asked.

"Once upon a time, years ago. Until my parents wanted

different things for me, and I changed my career." Unexpectedly, her eyes sharpened, her lips narrowed and the unpleasant expression I'd grown accustomed to settled on her face. "You don't think I could do it now, do you? Dance?"

Technically, that was a trick question. If I said yes, I would be berated for being insensitive to her advancing age. If I said no, then I'd be saying I thought she was too old to perform. How old was she, anyway? She had the ageless look that could pass for someone in her sixties, but also only be in her early forties.

I must have narrowed my eyes as I tried to figure it out, because she snapped, "What are you staring at me like that for?"

Immediately, I jerked my gaze to the ground and then felt even more obvious looking away. My eyes jumped around, trying to find something to get me out of trouble, before finally settling on her face again.

She harrumphed. "I've got better things to do than to stand here with you staring like a google-eyed imbecile."

"Sorry," I stammered, stepping back. My emotions flew around like a grandma's crazy quilt— half- embarrassed, half-irritated, and more than half offended at being called an imbecile. But insults came with the territory, especially when having to please a difficult customer.

At that, Steve got the safety bar down.

"Have a good afternoon." I could hardly wait to get into the suite and shut the door behind me. That woman. Ugh.

The room was dark with all the curtains closed. I fumbled for the switch on the wall and flipped it. The curtains opened with a whirring sound, and a rectangle of daylight fell across the floor and slowly grew, stretching over Dayton's suitcase, clothes strewn about the leather couch, the table, chairs, and finally... the bed.

One pale foot stuck out from the covers. My hand flew over my mouth. I'd seen enough dead bodies to recognize its waxy appearance.

Steve's eyes grew like eggs as he goggled between me and the bed. "Is he—?" He swallowed hard. "Mr. Dayton," he called. His voice cracked at the end. He said a little more forcefully, "Sir!"

I tip-toed over like I was cornering a mouse. I really didn't want to see what I knew I was about to. Fishing into my pocket for my phone, I took a deep breath to prepare myself. Two more steps and I was there.

Mr. Dayton was indeed deceased. He'd died with his eyes open, and they stared up at the ceiling. I shivered.

"Uh," Steve began. He turned then and ran to the bathroom. I could hear him vomiting. It was always the big guys.

I dialed 911 and called for help.

CHAPTER 5

About fifteen minutes later, I heard rattling in the hall. I went out to see two paramedics headed toward the room. Mrs. Richardson's door opened again.

"What's going on?" Her eyes narrowed suspiciously.

"It's a private matter. Guest confidentiality. But everything is taken care of." I smiled firmly and turned my back. Critic or not, I had to be in charge of the situation. Looky-lou's had to be discouraged.

"Excuse me?" she asked. But I ignored her and followed the paramedics into the room.

There was no sense of urgency. One paramedic did a preliminary examination with a stethoscope while the other shook out a long sheet.

"Any guesses as to the cause of death?" I asked.

The paramedic with the sheet walked over. "Obviously, there's no way for us to know for certain what happened, but given that he was found in bed, a likely theory would be cardiac arrest."

The two wine bottles by the bed jumped out at me. *Had it been alcohol poisoning? He hadn't seemed that drunk last night. Am I responsible if it was a heart attack? He said his heart was pounding last night. I should have insisted that the hotel call for an ambulance even when he said no.* I was kicking myself for not getting medical help.

"Ms. Swenson?" The paramedic set down the sheet. He waited for my response.

"I'm sorry, I'm just a little overwhelmed. He was acting a little irrational last night. He called me to his room a little after nine p.m. and insisted there'd been someone in his suite." I walked over to the side table and looked among the wine bottles for any prescription bottles. "I think, to be on the safe side, I'm going to need to call the police."

"Couldn't hurt," he shrugged. He probably wondered why I'd call for a drunkard who'd had a heart attack. The hotel had sadly seen more than its fair share of deaths over the years.

But what was gnawing at me was Dayton's insistence that

someone had been in the room. Of course I knew that was impossible, but still....

Still what? My inner voice pressed.

Still, I couldn't afford to ignore Dayton's claim, no matter how irrational the fear seemed to be. Not when the man died.

"How long do you think he's been... gone?" I asked.

The paramedic shrugged. "Not for me to say. Seems like it's been a while though."

I pulled out my phone to text Kristi Bentley.

Kristi was the sister of my best friend, Ruby, and she was also a sergeant for the Starke Springs police department. She was a force to be reckoned with and excellent at her job. Above all, she understood my need for discretion.

My fingers flew over the keyboard. —**Need the police to come. We have a DOA.**

She didn't text back. Instead, the phone buzzed with her incoming call. I appreciated it. I would have called her first, but I never knew what she was doing at her job.

"Maisie? What's up?" she asked.

"One of the hotel's guest failed to check out this afternoon. We've opened the room and discovered that he's deceased."

"Okay?" She sounded a little frustrated. Obviously, she *had* been busy when I texted.

"The problem is that he was quite irrational last night. He kept insisting that someone had been in his room and had woken him up earlier. I had security go through the suite and it was clear, but he was so upset I set up a guard outside his room."

"Any drug use?"

"Possibly. But nothing I can see off hand. I just need to cover my bases. The paramedics are getting ready to take him away right now."

"Any signs of violence?"

"I can't tell. Nothing that I can see." I was starting to feel foolish.

"Got it. I'm not far from you so I'll be there in a few minutes. Don't have them do anything more and don't you move anything." She hesitated, before adding, "But you know that already."

"I'll be good, mother," I said to tease her. She snorted and said goodbye.

The paramedics had been eavesdropping, and they'd already stepped away from the body and had started to pack their things.

"Where are you going?" I asked, sliding the phone into my pocket.

The first one answered me. "You've got the police on their way, so now the coroner needs to come get him."

I nodded and resisted fanning my face. The room felt overly hot. This wasn't really happening right next door to the hotel critic, was it? What were the odds?

The other paramedic latched the medical bag closed and chucked it on the stretcher while paramedic number one folded the sheet. Together, they left the suite.

The room was silent except for a ticking from somewhere. Even the normal street noise didn't carry up to the floor this high. I glanced at the bed, suddenly feeling very alone.

"Steve!" I yelled.

"Here," he hollered back. He sat slumped on the floor next to the door to the back half of the suite where the closet and bathroom were.

"You doing okay?" I wandered over and squatted next to him. He wasn't quite as green looking as he'd been earlier, but his lips were still white.

"Fine," he croaked.

"You want to head out?" I really didn't want him to leave me alone, but at the same time, the poor guy was really suffering.

"I'll leave when you leave," he said, slowly rising to his feet. He caught a glimpse of Mr. Dayton and slid back down the wall like an ice cube on a hot griddle.

"You sure about that?" I asked.

His face fell into his hands and his reply was muffled.

"What did you say?" I pushed his shoe with my foot.

"I said, I never thought I'd have to guard a dead guy."

A firm knock on the door interrupted my response. I opened it to reveal Kristi and her partner, Ryan Marshall. Mrs. Richardson was in the hallway behind them. She'd recently changed into a swimsuit and held a stack of towels, obviously on her way to the pool.

"Wow, you guys were quick," I said, opening the door wider to let the police officers in. Ryan entered and I could hear him talk with Steve.

"You sure everything is okay in there?" Mrs. Richardson asked, her voice low with suspicion.

"Everything's taken care of," I said with a wave.

Kristi gave her a measured stare which Mrs. Richardson seemed to gladly return. The tension between them built like a Jack-in-the-box that was about to go off. *Dear heavens, Kristi. Please do not take on the hotel critic!*

I cleared my throat and touched my friend's shoulder. "You ready?"

Kristi passed me slowly and entered the suite. Her eyebrow arched as she caught my eye.

I shut the door as quickly as I could behind her without being rude. My gut told me something was about to fly out of Kristi's mouth.

I wasn't disappointed. The door had barely clicked closed when Kristi blurted with a huff. "She seems overly interested. I don't trust her."

"She's a difficult guest," I said, like that was an explanation for Mrs. Richardson's curiosity.

"Difficult?" That word interested Kristi. She crossed her arms over her chest and waited.

"Yeah. She's a hotel critic my boss warned us was coming. And like all her predecessors, she's rude and demanding, and generally has all of us on pins and needles."

Kristi nodded understandingly. "I'm sure you guys will do fine."

"It's just my luck that her room happens to be next to the

dead body," I said glumly. "It's my fault. I upgraded her to that one for free when she checked in."

"Well, people do die," Kristi said, turning toward the bed. She cracked her fingers. "Now let's see about this body."

Steve moaned from his spot by the wall.

"You can leave," I said to him.

He swallowed hard as he gratefully nodded to me. The relief spilled off of him like a waterfall as he ran out of the room.

Kristi pulled a pair of black gloves from her back pocket and stretched them on. She walked over to the side of the bed where Ryan was already poking through one of the drawers.

She leaned to examine Mr. Dayton's hand. "Looky, looky. Now there's a cookie," she muttered.

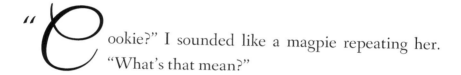

"ookie?" I sounded like a magpie repeating her. "What's that mean?"

Ryan leaned over the bed to check out what Kristi was referring too. He nodded grimly. "We better bag them up."

"Hey, guys?" I felt like an eight-year-old hanging out with my older sister's high school friends. "What's so interesting?"

"See his nails?" Kristi used a penlight to illuminate his fingertips more than the overhead light could. "They're all clipped short."

I was very disappointed. *Seriously?* "Well, I mean, I used to bite mine, but I clip them now myself."

"It's usually a sign of foul play. From a very smart criminal," she said.

I raised my brows.

She sighed and continued, speaking like I *was* that eight-year-old. "DNA is known to collect under nails. So clipped nails often means that the perpetrator is trying to prevent any possible DNA—specifically from them—from being exposed. Ryan, did you see any nail clippers?"

"None so far," he said, flashing the beam of his Maglight around.

"Keep an eye for that, and also nail shavings." Kari continued her examination.

"How do you know he didn't just clip them?" I asked.

Kristi flashed the light over his face. I winced at the sight. "See there? He's got quite the stubble going on. And check out his feet. Long toenails. Doesn't seem like trimming his fingernails is in keeping with his current hygiene practices."

I nodded, starting to feel worried. "Last night, he asked the front desk for me, so I came up here with Mike, one of our security guys. Dayton insisted that someone had been in his room and woken him up. He thought it was a ghost. We searched but there was no one here. Dayton was so freaked out that I went ahead and had Mike stand guard all night just for Dayton's peace of mind."

Kristi gave a firm nod at my explanation. "Well, we don't know anything yet. The coroner could still rule his death as one of natural causes. But I'm going to start gathering evidence just in case it's ruled otherwise." She flashed the penlight over the bed and then pulled back the top cover.

The light shone over the pillow under his head. Something about the pillow looked odd to me, but I couldn't figure out why.

Ryan headed for the bathroom as Kristi opened the bedside drawer, causing a pen inside to rattle around.

"You finding anything, Marshall?" she called.

"A bottle of pain reliever," Ryan answered.

"Ask him if he sees a tiny brandy bottle," I said.

"What brandy bottle?" Kristi flicked a sheet back and examined Dayton's body.

"Well, last night there was a hotel courtesy bottle and a glass sitting there." I pointed.

Kristi followed my gesture toward the table and then called to her partner who was still in the bathroom. "Marshall! You see any cups in there?"

"Yeah. A dirty coffee mug that has a cigar mashed out in it."

"Nothing else? A small brandy bottle?"

"That'd be a negative."

She gave me a curious look and then headed back to the closet alcove to see for herself. Of course, I followed. All I saw at the counter was the coffee station which held another coffee mug and a basket filled with flavored creamers and sugars. Next to that were four paper-wrapped drinking glasses.

My eyebrows flew up.

Kristi gestured at them with her penlight. "How many cups does the hotel stock in each room?"

"Four. But I know I saw one last night."

"Hmm. You think he could have washed and re-wrapped it?"

"Maybe?" But in my gut, I knew that was impossible. Dayton had been beside himself with anxiety. And, judging by the condition of his clothing, he hardly seemed like the type who would clean a used glass.

But it *was* possible that the unexplained presence of it sitting on the table—unexplained at least to him—bothered him enough that he wanted to put it back where it belonged.

Kristi raised an eyebrow at me. "You met him. Yes or no?"

I shrugged. "I can't answer that. I know I saw a glass last night, along with a bottle of brandy. Dayton insisted someone other than him had been in his room and drank it. And that person woke him up by touching his face."

Kristi turned toward the windows.

"They don't open," I said, guessing what she was thinking. "Mike went out on the balcony when we came up, but there was no one there. I can't see how someone would get on the balcony, anyway."

"Did Dayton say if the door was locked? Is it possible he lost his pass-key?"

"He said his door was locked." I frowned, realizing I should have asked about the pass-key. How could I have missed that? "I'm not sure about the pass-key, but when we came in this morning, the safety lock was on."

Kristi pulled open the drawer and pointed inside. "There are two keys in here. Marshall! Bag those cups on the counter, okay?"

"So you think he did wash the cup?" I asked.

She ignored my question and asked another one of her own. "You found him, right?"

"Well, Steve and I did."

"How did he appear?"

"What do you mean? Like he looks now. Dead. I tried not to look too close."

"Look at this, Benton. Found it in the bathroom trash." Ryan shook a bottle of pills where it sounded like just a few remained. "Prescription sleeping aid." He read the label. "And a strong one at that."

"Hmm, that makes sense," Kristi said after studying them.

"Sense how?" I asked. I was probably annoying them but I couldn't help it.

"You mix those with alcohol and you're in for a world of hallucinations," she said. "Ghosts, ghouls, and spookies in the night."

"So that combo could make him think that someone woke him up?" I asked.

"It sure can. Plus it induces amnesia. You said your security guy checked this room. From everything I've seen, I can confirm that there's no way in or out, other than by that door. And you had a guard standing there all night?"

"Yes," I said.

"Then most likely Dayton died of causes probably due to the mixture of the medication and alcohol."

"He'd said his heart was pounding. I asked him if he wanted an ambulance which he declined," I said. "He seemed sober enough to make that decision. But he was very paranoid."

"There's nothing you can do about that. He made his own choice." Kristi stared down at the body. "It appears he chose wrong."

"But what about the nails?" I pointed to where Dayton's hands lay curled on the sheet.

She shrugged. "Coincidences do sometimes happen on this job."

The coroner and his team arrived at that moment. I was surprised by how young the coroner looked. He slapped Ryan on the back and whistled as he examined the body.

Ryan filled the coroner in while the team bagged Dayton's hands and lifted him onto the gurney. Dayton's legs, clad in the same dark sweatpants I'd seen on him last night, were wooden-like. His one hand stayed clenched in the air as if it were still resting on the blanket. I turned away, my stomach flip-flopping, feeling more empathy with Steve than ever.

As the coroner worked, he spoke his impressions into a tiny voice recorder. I caught one of them. "Rigor mortis observed in the upper half and nearly completely through the lower extremities. Cautious time of death, two a.m." He clicked it off and whistled again.

Two of the coroner's team hefted Dayton up onto the stretcher. The coroner scribbled on a clipboard as the team buckled the body down. He dropped his pen, and I bent down to get it.

"Thanks," he said with a wink and gave me a slow smile.

Inwardly, I groaned. Was he flirting with me? Over a dead body?

"No problem," I muttered and moved away.

The team finished buckling Dayton on and then covered him, head to toe, with a thick blanket.

I dialed Steve who was down in the lobby. "We're about to come down. Make sure the elevator and foyer are clear of guests and then get back to me."

I hung up, and we gathered at the door. The stretcher squeaked as the coroner's team jimmied it so they could push it through the door once we got word.

We silently stood there like we were waiting for some grand marshal's whistle to start a morbid parade.

A few minutes later, Steve called back. "All clear, boss."

"Everything good?" Kristi asked, turning the doorknob.

I nodded. She held the door open as the coroner's team wheeled Dayton out. Together, we headed down the hall.

There was a service elevator that I would have preferred to use, but it wasn't quite big enough to hold the stretcher. I followed the team to one of the main elevators and stuck in my key to over-ride any stop requests from the other floors. We made it down to the ground floor without incident, and the coroner and his team, along with Kristi and her partner, left without further incident.

There were a few rubberneckers outside, but Steve and the rest of the security had done a great job in keeping everyone back.

The body was loaded and, finally, the coroner drove away. I breathed a sigh of relief, hoping that was the last I would ever hear about Mr. Dayton.

CHAPTER 7

Some days have a string of events that happen like a line of dominoes falling down. Today was definitely one of those days. I was only half-way back to my office when the next domino fell, in the form of a phone call.

It was Julie from housekeeping.

I frowned as I answered it, wondering what new appliance was now being used for hotel room cooking. Who knows, maybe they were making grilled cheese with the hair dryer.

"Hi, Julie," I said.

"Ms. Swenson, the linen order you made came in."

Hmm. Why was there still no chipper tone to her voice?

"Great!" I responded, hoping my enthusiasm would prompt hers.

That hope would be a negative. Her tone sounded even more depressed. "There's a problem. Can you come down to the laundry room?"

I bit back a groan. "Absolutely. I'll be down in just a minute." I was already heading out of the office before we hung up.

As I walked to the hotel's laundry center, I was slightly upset with myself for my choice of shoes. They were pointy, with heels that bit into my toes, and my feet were starting to kill me. I needed to dig out my sandals.

The laundry room was bustling with rumbling machines and workers when I entered. The entire room seemed to be powered solely by the scents of fabric softener and bleach. Washers roared around me. Dryers thumped. In the far corner, a column of steam rose. I spotted Julie by the folding area, which was several long white tables set up next to shelves of sheets, pillows, and blankets. I headed over there.

As I approached, I could see the problem, and my steps slowed. Before her, like a mighty snow fortress built to tipping height, was a mountain of pillows. There were even more pillows stacked on the table behind her, spilling onto the floor.

"Ms. Swenson, what did you do?" The short woman's face

was etched with deep lines by her mouth. "Over seven hundred pillows, Ms. Swenson." She picked one up and shook it. The pillow puffed in plushness.

My mouth dropped. I turned a slow circle, wide-eyed, at the mounds of pillows on the floor. The sheer number made me wilt inside. "I didn't order any pillows. You told me sheets so I ordered an extra eighty sheets."

"Here's the order slip." Julie handed me a yellow paper. I quickly scanned it. Seven hundred and twelve pillows, just like she said. *What in the world is going on?*

My gaze skipped down the list to land on the hotel name.

OceanSprings.

"Wait a minute," I said, ballooning back up with relief. "The company mixed our name with someone else's. This was their mistake."

"That's all fine and dandy, but now what am I supposed to do with them?" Julie's hands hung limply at the sides of her white starched uniform.

"Don't worry. I'll take care of it," I assured her. "In the meantime, where are the boxes they came in?"

She shook her head. "The night crew incinerated them."

I wrinkled my nose. The one time I wished my staff wasn't

quite so efficient.

"I do like them though," Julie said, running her hand across the surface. "Not only are they hypoallergenic, but they're made with that new poly-fill that actually improves with machine washing."

Hmm. Well, that was something to consider. I tested the fill myself by pressing my hand into it. Very soft.

I stared at the dent my hand left in the pillow, suddenly reminded of something.

"What are you going to do about it?" Julie asked, knocking me out of my musing.

I blinked, pulling myself out of my thoughts. "I'm on it. For now, just stack them over there. I'll see if I can track down something to vacuum-seal them into bags." With the order form firmly in my hand, I pulled my phone out and dialed the linen supply company.

They, of course, were very apologetic and promised to correct the mistake within twenty-four hours. I hoped our limited reserve of sheets would last that long or I'd be making a run to the home supply store to pick up some new ones.

The imprint of my hand on the pillow still bothered me as I walked back to the front desk and into the stock office to get some coffee. What was it that bothered me so much about it?

The thought kept slipping out of reach like trying to reach for a minnow in a lake.

I decided to leave it alone and started to puzzle over how to fix the coffee pot problem and the battle I had on my hands to get Mr. Phillips to switch to a new coffee system.

It was then that it happened. Somehow, by not thinking about the pillow, the answer popped into my mind.

Mr. Dayton. When he'd been laying in bed, there'd been a very similar indent in the pillow next to his head. *How would you get a deep imprint like that if you weren't leaning into the pillow?*

This made me think of the coroner, the guy who eyed me much too long over a dead body. But one thing that he'd muttered into his recorder nagged at me too. He'd estimated the time of death at two a.m.

But Mike had said he'd spoken to Dayton this morning. He said the guest had actually opened the door.

Could the coroner be that far off? How was that possible? Surely, he wouldn't make that big of an error.

I took a sip of coffee, considering. It was funny how you never thought of these things at the time when you could actually ask for an explanation. A glance at the wall clock said it was five p.m. Mike was probably home in bed, sleeping. I remember working the night schedule myself in my early twenties, and it could be brutal.

Still, I needed to talk with him so I sent him a text. —**Call me as soon as you wake up.**

Then I texted Kristi and asked her to call me when she was free. After I sent it, I stared at the phone, half-expecting it to ring. But when it didn't, I continued to my office where an enormous stack of messages—everything from meat shortages in the kitchen, to a PR company wanting access to the hotel to make a commercial—waited for me to sort out.

It was actually several hours later when my phone finally rang. I glanced blearily from the computer screen to the phone.

Kristi.

"Hey, lady," I answered. I stretched my tired muscles.

"You rang?"

"I had a few thoughts I wanted to go over with you from this morning. Did you by chance hear the coroner mention that the possible time of death was at two a.m.?"

"Yes. On account of the degree of rigor mortis he observed."

I wrinkled my nose at the thought. "Well, there's a problem with that."

"What's the problem?"

I deflected her question with one of my own. "Is there anything else that can mimic that stiffness? Like a drug overdose or a seizure? Because Mike, our security guy, actually spoke face to face with Dayton this morning."

"Actually talked with him? What time was this? And, no, Maisie. There's nothing that mimics rigor mortis. It's kind of a dead thing."

I rolled my eyes. Kristi had always been sarcastic, even while growing up.

"Well, it's not like I'm a mortician or something," I shot back.

Kristi snorted. "That's a fact. Now get back to what you were saying about this morning security-talk business."

"Our security guy knocked on Dayton's door at around eight this morning to check on him. Mike wanted to let Dayton know he was leaving."

"You're telling me that Mike had visual verification that Dayton was alive and well?"

"Yep."

"That's a problem." Her voice was crisp.

I couldn't help feeling pleased she'd been convinced. "So, is it possible that some kind of drug caused that reaction?"

"Mimic rigor mortis? I can't imagine." Her voice trailed away as she seemed to be considering it. Finally, "I'll be interested in hearing the final conclusions from the coroner. Hopefully, he'll get back to us sooner than later."

"Don't hang up yet," I said. "I also wanted to bring up something else I thought was weird."

An extra long exhale came from the other end.

"What?" I asked.

"You just strung two words together that make me nervous. Thinking, and weird. I'm afraid to ask what's going on in that head of yours."

"I'm serious. Remember when we found him? You flashed the light over his face, and I noticed the pillow looked puffed and perfect, except for a huge impression on one side. I made that same exact dent by leaning on a pillow this afternoon. So how did that dent get there? And don't forget, you *did* say his fingernails were clipped."

"All right. I get it. You think there could be foul play. Don't worry because we're still digging into it even if it's being considered an O.D. for the time being. The first step is that coroner's report. So hang tight and don't do any more poking around."

"You got it," I said, and we hung up. I glanced at the clock.

Seven o'clock. This day had flown by, and I was starving. I headed out of my office and locked the door behind me.

The lobby was filled with families returning from their day. Sunburns glowed on most of their cheeks and many of the kids wore ear hats and had arms full of won prizes. Another river of people headed down the hall to the hotel's restaurant, which would be busy until late at night. And, in a few hours, there would be another deluge of guests leaving since the theme park had a nightly fireworks show.

Guests were like the tide, constantly coming and going. My hands clasped behind my back and I smiled as I watched my employees intermingle with the guests, give general directions, and replace lost room keys.

Jennifer Parkins, the guest who'd earlier been so impressed with the complimentary breakfast, bumped into me. There was an awkward moment as I tried to pull my foot out from under hers, hating my pointy shoes even more.

"Oops! I'm so sorry!" Her face flushed.

Foot freed, I grinned to reassure her. "No worries. Jennifer. How are you doing this evening?"

"Oh fine. Fine. You sure your foot is okay?"

I wiggled it so she could see for herself it was working.

A relieved expression brightened her eyes, and she gave a

toothy grin. "I'm so clumsy sometimes. Can you believe I once broke my arm falling off a bunk bed, and right after it healed, broke the other one rollerskating? I swear I almost gave my mom a nervous break-down growing up."

I laughed, being able to relate. "I was in fast pitch and have a few stories of my own. Naturally, my mom likes to trot them out to embarrass me."

"Mothers." She rolled her eyes. "Mine's back in Chicago, probably bundled up in her sweater and a blanket. Speaking of the weather, it's a beautiful night here in Starke Springs, isn't it? Positively balmy. Gives me a chance to wear my new sari." She grasped the fabric and did a little twirl.

"And that looks absolutely lovely on you," I said.

The plump woman giggled. "I purchased it down at Key West last year. Never felt quite comfortable to wear it. But then I thought to myself, what do I have to lose? Who am I trying to impress?"

"That's a great attitude to have." I nodded. "Sometimes we worry way too much about what others think. So tell me, did you get a chance to enjoy the ocean? What plans do you—"

My comment was interrupted by a raised voice calling my name. "Ms. Swenson!"

I turned to see a very angry looking Mrs. Richardson. She

marched into the foyer from the direction of the restaurant, her cheeks puffed with indignation.

"Excuse me," I said to Jennifer and hurried over to meet Mrs. Richardson half-way before she could make a scene. What on earth was going on now?

"Mrs. Richardson, how can I help you?" I asked.

"You call that 'exquisite dining'?" she huffed. Her nose seemed even sharper as she stared down it.

My eyebrows rose, but I didn't respond, choosing instead to give her space to make her complaint.

And she was happy to seize the moment. With her hands on her hips, she blasted out, "Medium-rare! Is that so hard? Not medium, not rare. Medium-rare."

I blinked. "Were you able to address this with your waiter?"

"I shouldn't have to." She fumed, her thin lips squeezing together.

My phone buzzed in my pocket, indicating a phone call. But how to answer it without riling Mrs. Richardson up more?

I pulled it out and glanced at the number. Mike. With impatience prickling like a buzzing mosquito, I waited for Mrs. Richardson to take a breath so I could cut in.

Finally, it came. "I'm terribly sorry, Mrs. Richardson. I need to take this. It's the Governor. Allow me to get someone to make this right with you." I glanced at the front desk and was sorry to see the sweetest clerk, Clarissa, busy with a guest. I gestured Sierra to come over. She saw Mrs. Richardson and formed the fakest smile I'd ever seen as she walked over.

Sierra was very efficient but was also known for not putting up with any flack. I hoped my wild eyes projected the need that Mrs. Richardson had to be coddled and appeased.

"Mrs. Richardson," Sierra dipped her head in the older woman's direction.

"I'm leaving you in capable hands," I said, lifting the phone to my ear. I hoped I really was. It seemed like a black cloud was over this whole woman's stay.

"Hello?" I said into the phone as I hurried for my office.

"Ms. Swenson?"

"Hi, Mike. I wasn't expecting to get a call back so soon." I hesitated, not wanting to shock him. "Have you heard from the police?"

"The police? What for?" Shocked. Apparently, I failed at my 'softening the blow' technique.

Might as well rip off the rest of the band-aid. "Mr. Dayton was found deceased this afternoon."

"What?" The word was uttered in the harshest whisper. I waited a few seconds to let him digest that information.

"I just talked to him this morning," he finally said.

"Yes, that's what I needed to discuss with you. And to give you a heads up that the police will probably want to as well. Now, can you tell me again what exactly happened during your guard duty? Did you hear anything weird during the night?"

"You're scaring me. What do you mean, did I hear anything weird? Was there really someone in the room with him?"

"No, no. Nothing like that. But I'm double-checking after the strange statements he was throwing around last night. So, any weird thumps or noises?"

"Uh, no. He was actually really quiet the entire time. I figured he went straight to bed."

"And this morning, can you tell me again what happened before you left?"

"It, uh, it was time for my shift to end. I wanted to let Mr. Dayton know, but the idea of waking him kind of made me feel bad. But then I did hear some movement, so I went ahead and knocked."

"Movement?"

"Yeah, just some normal stuff. A drawer opening and closing."

"Okay, and then what happened?"

"He, uh, he opened the door, and I said, 'Hey, it's Mike and my shift's over. Just letting you know I'm leaving. Everything good in there?' And he said. "Everything's fine. I'm just finished packing now. Thanks.' And then the door closed."

Something about Mike's statement bothered me. What was it?

"How did he seem?" I asked.

"He seemed tired. Groggy like maybe he didn't get enough sleep."

"Why do you think that?"

"His, uh, his voice was deep and muffled."

The bothered feeling poked me like a hot iron. "His voice? But what about his appearance? What was that like?"

Mike cleared his throat. I waited for an answer.

Nothing.

"Mike?"

"Uh, he never opened his door past the safety lock. I guess I didn't actually see his face."

My eyes flew wide open. "Don't you think that detail is sort of important? You have to share that with the police because they're setting the time of death based on you being the last person to have seen him. But you didn't see him after all. That person at the door could have been anyone."

"Anyone?" he asked. "Ms. Swenson, I was right outside the door the entire night. How could anyone have gotten in?"

That was true. And on the thirty-first floor, it was absurd to think of someone climbing up to the balcony. Besides, wouldn't Mike have heard if anyone had tried to break the sliding glass door?

"You never left?" I asked.

"No. Not even once."

I bit my lip. It had to have been Dayton talking to Mike then. He must have just been groggy or hung-over. Maybe Dayton had been embarrassed by the way he'd acted the night before, and that's why he didn't open the door all the way. The coroner had to be wrong about the time.

"Okay, thanks for getting back to me so quickly. I'm going to pass this on to the officer on the case," I said.

"Want me to come in early?"

"No, you're fine. I'll see you later tonight."

CHAPTER 8

*A*s soon as I got off the phone with Mike, I texted Kristi to share the news: —**The suite's door had opened, but Mike didn't actually see Mr. Dayton.** I ended my message with—**but Mike guarded that room all night. There's no way anyone could have gotten in!**

Her text back was more to the point. —**You'd never believe how ingenious people can be. BTW We've notified the next of kin. They'll be by to pick up his items.**

Terrific. I glanced at the clock and sighed. Nearly eight pm. I'd managed to miss lunch, and now dinner. No rest for the weary, I guess. I wearily stood up to go get Dayton's stuff ready for the next of kin.

But first, I headed to the workroom behind the front desk and picked a sandwich from the vending machine. It dispensed with a clunk. I swear my knees creaked when I bent down to get it. I peeled back the cellophane from the plastic container and a pickle fell out, but I caught it. No way was I going to waste a pickle.

I took a bite and dialed Michelle, the night supervisor of the laundry center.

"Hi, Ms. Swenson,"

"Hi, Michelle. Do you have a few minutes to come pack up a room with me?"

"Oh." Michelle was a young mom with a long blonde braid that fell nearly to her waist. Her voice lowered in a show of sympathy. "Is it that the poor guy I heard had a heart attack this morning?"

"Yep." The prospect of the chore ahead of me folding the clothing that had been strewn all over the suite made me want to about drop.

I suddenly straightened. *Wait a minute. Hadn't Mike said that Mr. Dayton told him he was finished packing?*

Michelle clucked her tongue. "Absolutely, Ms. Swenson. It's terrible that happened."

Mentally, I agreed. It was cold-hearted, but the thought crossed my mind that it couldn't have happened on a worse day with the hotel reviewer right next door. "I'll meet you up there."

I headed out of the workroom, feeling like the time when I'd tried my first Zumba class and discovered that I had no rhythm what-so-ever, even with an instructor calling out the beats. It had taken all my energy just to fake the moves, and I'd been so exhausted at the end that I'd treated myself to a glorious piece of lime cheesecake at one of my favorite restaurants. That type of exhaustion was what I was dealing with now.

And I was craving cheesecake.

Charlotte, our night receptionist, was zoning out in front of what looked suspiciously like a computer game flashing on her screen. A man entered through the hotel's revolving doors.

Normally, a lone guest's entrance would make about as much of an impact on my radar as a leaf in a windstorm. But right behind him were two other men dressed in long overcoats. The men in coats broke off and stood at the entrance.

That caught my attention.

He wore a fedora hat and Hawaiian shirt, not uncommon for our area. He was also one of those terminal sunglass wearers. The dark shades covered half his face. He zeroed in on me like a hummingbird to a red flower and a big smile spread across his face. His arms opened in eagerness to envelop me in a hug.

"Ms. Swenson!" he said, his voice dripping with honey.

I honestly didn't know what to do. Who was this strange guy? I glanced around, but of course, none of my hotel's security was visible. My sole help was Rob the bellhop, a kid who'd just turned seventeen and whose body mass hadn't quite caught up with his lanky height.

Just you and me here, Rob. Look lively.

"Yes, that's me. How can I help you?" I asked, throwing my arm forward for a stiff handshake and to create space between us.

The man stopped and stared at my hand like it was a dead rat. "Ms. Swenson, I *am* a hugger."

I smiled grimly. "Allow me to shake your hand this time and formally meet."

"I am Mr. Stephenson, Vincent Dayton's brother."

I must have looked confused at the different last name because he continued. "Half-brothers. We're all that's left of our family." His animated features immediately fell into an expression of sorrow. The clash was so disjointing that I had a hard time registering that he was, indeed, a blood relative.

"I heard you were the one who found poor Vincent?" he asked, his eyebrows creasing together, forming two red lines.

"Yes, I am. I'm so sorry."

"Ahh, life." He waved his hand dramatically. "Tis but a bit of honeycomb to be enjoyed in the moment. Every bit of sweetness must be sucked out." He lowered his sunglasses and stared at me over the top. "Because, in the end, you're only left with an empty husk."

I swallowed hard.

"At any rate," his breezy attitude returned. "I'm here to collect his items. They are in his room, yes?"

"I was just on my way to pack them. If you'd like, you can wait at the Oceanside's restaurant until I've finished. Order whatever you want, compliments of the hotel." I glanced at the two thugs by the door. "Your guests are included as well, of course."

"Oh, no. I wouldn't want to trouble you. Allow me to go up to the room and Joe over there can pack." He jerked his thumb toward one of the thugs.

"If I can just see some ID," I said. "And there will be forms to fill out."

He whipped off the sunglasses completely this time and began polishing them. "ID? I'm not sure I have that on me at the moment. I've never needed it before. Gordo drives me around. He takes care of everything." He slipped the glasses back on and snapped his fingers. One of the goons, presumably the said 'Gordo' waltzed over.

"Gordo, you have my ID?" Mr. Stephenson asked out of the corner of his mouth.

The goon reached into his pocket and pulled out a wallet. He handed it to Mr. Stephenson, who opened it to reveal a thick wad of bills. Mr. Stephenson's thumb ruffled them softly as he stared at me, his glasses giving the appearance of sightless eyes.

"Will this work for now?" he asked. "I can stop by tomorrow with the real deal. Promise."

"Err..." I was slightly stunned. "Let me go ahead and get everything packed up. I'll have it waiting for you down at the desk tomorrow."

He snapped the wallet shut and handed it back to the bodyguard. "I see. Well, there's some important papers Vincent was telling me about. Very important. Let me at least pick those up so they don't get lost. I know how things can get chaotic."

My heart did a double-beat. Good grief. How in the world had I forgotten about Dayton's envelope in the safe? My surprise must have shown on my face because Mr. Stephenson stuck his tongue in his cheek and stared up at the ceiling like he was unimpressed.

He dragged his gaze slowly back to me. "Don't be difficult," he advised, his voice low and measured. "I don't like it when people are difficult. Besides, you're a sweetheart. You need to smile more. Be a shame to see anything happen to make you not smile."

My mouth went dry. "Mr. Stephenson, I have to work by the hotel's policy and—"

"Who's the boss around here?" His head swiveled as if he were really searching. "Let me talk to the big guy."

"That would be me," I answered stiffly.

"Oh yeah?" He stepped back and appraised me from head to toe. "You're the boss lady? Hey, Joe, she's the boss lady. Wha'da ya think of that?"

From the doorway, Joe smirked in my direction.

Okay. Enough was enough. "Mr. Stephenson, with the police involved—"

"Whoa! Whoa! Whoa! Why you got to be like that? Who said anything about the police? No need to bring them into it."

"They're already in it," I said. "And we'll be doing this by the book. I'll have everything packed up for you when you return tomorrow with the proper identification. Again, I'm so sorry. There's nothing more I can do for you."

The short man scowled at me, but I wasn't budging. He must have surmised that because a second later he snapped his fingers. "Let's go, Gordo."

The huge guy followed after his boss, with Joe following behind them like the caboose as they pushed through the revolving door.

"Well," said Charlotte, who mysteriously appeared at my side. "That was interesting."

"You're telling me." I breathed out. "Okay, I'm heading upstairs. Let me know if they come back."

"Aye Aye, Captain." She gave me a mock salute and sauntered back to the front desk.

I hurried to the elevator and stabbed the up button. My mind replayed the conversation I'd first had with Mr. Dayton when he checked in. He'd been absolutely frantic about the safety of his leather envelope. The envelope with the specific instructions that it go to his lawyer in the unexpected event of his death.

How had his half-brother known about the envelope? Was it really his brother? I wondered if Mr. Stephenson would show up tomorrow with proper identification, and what would happen when I said I still couldn't release the envelope to him.

I rubbed my throat, remembering his leer when he'd talked about my smile. I really didn't want to find out what he would do.

But I was about to.

CHAPTER 9

*E*very wisp of my fatigue had vanished as I stomped down the hall to the 360 hotel suite. My steps were half-fueled with anxiety that there was more trouble ahead, and half from anger at the way Mr. Stephenson had tried to push me around.

Michelle was already waiting outside the suite with a cleaning supply cart and a cardboard box. What wouldn't fit in the suitcase would be boxed up for the next of kin.

I opened the door and flipped on the light. The room was in the same state of disarray that I'd remembered from that morning with the police. Dayton's clothing was strewn across the couch. There was a half empty bag of chips, two wine bottles, and more clothing on the tables and floor.

I walked into the alcove past the closet—noting that the ironing board was pulled down—and into the bathroom. Immediately, my eyes squeezed closed.

Housekeeping must be one of the most under-appreciated aspects of vacation travels. They dealt with things I never wanted to see, and without them, this hotel would be in shambles.

The first thing that hit me was the stench of vomit. Had Steve done that? The second, stale cigarette smoke. A coffee cup sat on the counter. Cigarette or maybe cigar ashes spilled about it. Peeking into the cup proved it was a cigar, dunked out in tobacco-colored water.

The toilet paper spindle held an empty cardboard roll. Two more rolls sat on the floor, each half-used as if Dayton couldn't decide which roll he liked better.

But the toilet. The toilet. It was covered in some type of body fluid. I gagged and backed away.

As I stepped back over the alcove threshold, my attention was caught by a clump of something on the floor. What was that? Hair? This man was disgusting.

"Sometimes a mask works the best," Michelle said from behind me, with a scarf over her face. "Or I use my scarf. I put peppermint oil in it."

I shuddered weakly. "I don't know how you do it," I admitted.

"I don't have a choice. I have a family to feed," she said, flipping her braid off her shoulder.

Stomach rolling, I walked back in the bedroom and lifted the suitcase onto the coffee table with a grunt. I unzipped it and flopped the top half open. The case was already semi-filled with clothes, none of them folded. Curiously, I examined the tag on the handle.

I bent closer to read it again. What was this? Milan? Didn't Dayton say he'd just flown back from Madrid? How had he mixed those up? Did he just get confused?

Eyeing the suitcase, I had half a mind to rifle through it and see what I could find. Maybe a clue to the real reason he died.

I glanced at the alcove and was startled to see Michelle standing in the doorway.

"What?" she asked. And then nodding to the suitcase. "I don't see anything. Besides, I have a mess to clean." With that, she walked back to her cart and wheeled it to the alcove. After checking that her scarf was firmly in place, she donned a pair of rubber gloves. With one of the cart's wheels squeaking, she entered the bathroom.

That woman deserves a raise.

I dragged my attention back to the suitcase. It was obviously expensive, the attention to detail impeccable. There were scuff marks on its corners to indicate heavy use.

Several of the inside compartments were zippered. I hesitated only a moment, and then unzipped one, reasoning that I needed to catalogue what I was giving to the half-brother, after all.

The first pocket contained a card from the Hotel La Habana with a phone number scrawled on the back. There were only eight digits, seeming to prove it was a foreign number. Seeing it made me glance around for Dayton's cell phone. Where was it at?

A sense of unease started to flare when I didn't spot it. Everyone had a phone now-a-days, and not finding his nearly made me interrupt what I was doing to go search for it. But instead, I continued my foraging.

The next pocket had some lint and a papery item. I pulled out the paper to see a cigar band. I slid it around my pinky to read it. Camacho. I wondered if the one in the bathroom was this brand. The yellow and black band brought back memories of my dad who at one point decided that he was a cigar aficionado. He tried it for a while before that fad lost its luster for him.

I put the cigar band on the coffee table and continued to explore the pockets. When there was nothing more of interest, I turned my attention to the contents inside. It was partially filled with jumbled up clothing. Obviously, he didn't care enough about what he owned other than to make them fit inside the case. There were a few polos and jeans, most worn soft from long years of wear. Underneath the pile was a pair of black jeans. They'd been rolled into a log and were stiff as though they'd just been purchased and hadn't gone through the wash yet. Crammed into the bottom was a button-up bright blue Oxford. I shook it out. Although wrinkled, it also appeared new.

Interesting.

Frowning, I replaced it and started in on the sweatpants slung over the back of the couch. A harsh bang, like the toilet lid being dropped, clanged from the bathroom. My heart squeezed with sympathy for Michelle.

I spotted a pair of dirty underwear under the table that impressed on me the need for my own rubber gloves. I went in search of the cart.

The bathroom was considerably cleaner in just the short time that I'd been packing. Michelle had a bottle of disinfectant and was spraying the walls around the toilet as if she were a graffiti artist. I snagged a pair of gloves and left.

As I passed the closet again, I spotted the ironing board again. Normally, the board was in an upright position in a pocket in the wall. It struck me as odd since all of Dayton's clothes were balled up and wrinkled. In fact, I wasn't sure I'd even seen anything that would need to be ironed as I was packing.

There was that one blue shirt, but it had the appearance of being forgotten the way it'd been balled up at the bottom of the suitcase.

Did he use the iron for bacon...?

After Julie brought the problem to me, I did some internet searching. She'd been right, there was a video about hotel cooking hacks that had gone viral. I walked over and checked the bottom of the iron for grease. Nothing. Feeling kind of silly, I brought it to my nose to sniff. It smelled more like the scent of scorched clothing than anything else.

Puzzled, I returned to the living room and folded more clothes.

Michelle came out with a plastic bag filled. "Toothpaste, a brush, a pair of socks, that sort of thing," she said as an explanation.

I opened the bedside table to make sure I wasn't missing anything. There was nothing inside but the Gideon bible. I was about to close the drawer when I noticed a corner of a piece of paper peeking out from between the pages of the bible. I pulled it out. It appeared to be a note.

I read out loud, "In the event of my death please give all my personal items, including the envelope in the hotel safe to my...."

The next line was the start of a cursive letter *A*. I turned my head trying to guess what it was for. Was he trying to write the word "attorney?" I tucked the letter and the plastic bag into the suitcase and closed it. It zipped with a little coaxing.

"All right, then." I brushed my hands off. "That's all ready for Mr. Stephenson. Assuming he comes back with the proper identification, that is." Remembering his interesting entrance, I decided to send a text to Kristi to ask if the name, Stephenson, rang a bell, just in case.

I heaved the suitcase off the couch and onto the floor. Something greasy from the handle smeared on my palm. It smelled like cinnamon. I had no idea what it was, but I was incredibly thankful I was still wearing the gloves.

Kristi wrote back. **—Leave everything alone. Forensics are on their way.**

I froze while reading it. And then furiously typed—**A little too late for that. We just packed the suitcase and Michelle is cleaning the bathroom as we speak**.

Kristi's response was immediate—**Stop!**

"Uh, Michelle!" I called, typing back. **—You told me to get the things ready for the next of kin?**

The housekeeper poked her head out, her face still swathed in the scarf. "Yeah, boss?" she muffled.

"We've got to stop cleaning. Apparently, the police want to search this room.

She rolled her eyes. "Always something. I did find this." She held out a half of a watch band.

The strap looked like it had been broken and was black and fairly thin. It was the piece that had the holes, and the fourth hole was clearly bigger with a worn line delineating where the metal clasp had been used.

"Where did you find this?" I asked.

"Just inside the bathroom entrance." She pointed a rubber-gloved hand in the direction she meant.

I set it on the nightstand, spotting my own rubber gloves. With a sigh, I rolled my eyes. We hadn't worn them the entire time we'd been in the suite, and with Kristi's demand, I was guessing both Michelle and I would be asked to come down to get fingerprinted.

I left the suitcase by the door and we left, Michelle pushing the cart. As I passed Mrs. Richardson's door, it sprung open.

"What kind of place is this? I've never seen the like of it." She looked down her sharp nose at me and tugged her bathrobe closed.

"Excuse me?" I asked. Michelle kept on going.

"What is it? A luxury hotel or a train station?"

I nodded, figuring she meant the police coming through. "I'm terribly sorry for today's distractions. Can I get you tickets to a comedy show? Derek Daniels is in town right now."

"It wasn't just today. There was noise all night."

"From next door?" My interest perked. What had she heard during the night?

Her brow wrinkled. "Next door? No. It was overhead. What is this place, a frat house?"

That reminded me that Dayton had said the same thing. Had it happened again? I needed to check on who was in that upstairs room. If those rowdy guests were there again tonight, I needed to move Mrs. Richardson. In fact, it might not be such a bad idea no matter what. "I'm so sorry. I wish you would have called the front desk. We could have stopped that."

She sniffed and slammed the door without a response. I resisted the urge to allow my shoulders to slump. I would win that woman over, one way or another.

CHAPTER 10

*F*inally, at nearly ten o'clock that night, I was able to crawl into bed. The scent of lavender fabric softener enveloped me as I pulled the covers up to my chin, promising, *"Tomorrow is a new day. Surely it will be better than today."*

It turned out, I really needed to quit making promises to myself.

I woke up in a cold sweat. It was pitch black, but all I could see was remnants of my nightmare. A magazine's front cover screaming, "OceanSide Hotel loses a star! Four stars, four stars only!"

I grabbed my phone, my hands trembling, needing to talk to my best friend (and Kristi's little sister.) Could I call her? My heart pounded. Of course, I could. Ruby was always there for me, and likewise me for her. Besides, it was only...two a.m. I swallowed hard and dialed anyway.

The phone was answered with a mumbled, "Ruby Bentley here. How can I help you?"

She worked in retail and obviously wasn't fully awake. "Ruby," I hissed. "It's me, Maisie."

"Maisie?" Her voice raised. "What's wrong? Where are you?"

"I'm in bed," I admitted. "I had a nightmare."

I heard shifting as she sat up. "A nightmare? Are you okay?"

"Yeah, but I had this horrible dream the hotel critic staying at our hotel right now knocked down our star rating. I'm terrified that will happen. It really could because I can't seem to win this woman over. Mr. Phillips threatened he might let go some of our employees if something like that does happen."

She snorted. "Maisie, he's just trying to turn the screws on your soft heart. He's not going to let any of the staff go. Why would he? Think about it."

"Because they're awesome?" I guessed at her answer.

"No. Because he's a penny pincher and all of his staff are well-trained and work as a team. He's not going to pay for extra training for new staff that will require over-time until they learn to get the work done."

"Oh. Yeah, that too."

"Go back to sleep. It's going to be okay. You wait and see."

"But this lady—"

"No buts. That critic-lady won't break the Oceanside. I can promise you that."

I hung up with a smile on my face. Sometimes it was nice to have a friend who knew you so well they could tell you to chill out, and you'd really listen.

THE NEXT MORNING started innocently enough. I took Bingo for a trip to the dog park and texted Ruby to thank her for the middle of the night counseling session. When I returned, I found Momma had made French toast. We had a great breakfast while she regaled me with tales about being paired up with Mr. Carmichael for Bridge during game night.

"But that woman is a hussy," Momma ended with a sniff.

"What on earth? Are you talking about Tawny Myers? Momma, that's not nice."

"Oh, I have stronger words than that! Hussy is me being polite."

"What happened?" I asked, taking a huge bite of syrupy toast.

"I went up to the refreshment table to refill my drink. When I came back, *she* was seated next to Mr. Carmichael. They were giggling over cards. And she wouldn't move."

"You're kidding me?"

"Nope, just eyed me under those spider legs she calls eyelashes before simpering again at something he said." She frowned at the memory. "Sounding like a hyena. A hussy hyena."

Coffee doesn't feel very good when shot out the nose. But darn it if Momma's word picture didn't make me snort while I was drinking. Served me right. I should have known better.

Momma stared at me while I grabbed a napkin to mop up.

"So what did you do?" I asked.

"Oh, I was polite. I asked her how she was feeling, and if her uncontrollable laughter was a side effect from the incontinence medicine she was using."

I swear, I almost snorted again. "Momma!"

She sipped with a wide-eyed expression. "What? Anyway, Tawny didn't answer, but she wrinkled her nose like she could smell a fly fart three miles away. I did catch Mr. Carmichael give her a side glance when she got up later. Of course, I took my seat back."

"And that was the end of it?"

"Oh, and I won."

"You won Bridge?"

"Bridge?" Two lines formed between her brows as if she were in deep thought. "I can't remember how the game ended." She gave me a wicked smile. "Now eat your toast. You need the energy. Who knows how many dead bodies you're going to find today."

"That's not even funny," I grumped, taking another bite.

Turns out, she wasn't that far off.

Before I finished my toast, I texted Sierra. —**Please send a complimentary ticket for the Laugh a Million show to Mrs. Richardson's room on behalf of the hotel.** Hopefully, that would cool the critic down. And the room above hers had new guests today, so she wouldn't have to deal with the same noise issue again.

As hurried to my office I made a mental note to check on the pillow issue. Hopefully, the sheets would be in today. Passing by the elevator brought me face-to-face with Jennifer Parkins, again. She was just exiting, along with a couple and their two young children. The family wore bathing suits, and I assumed they were on their way to enjoy the Oceanside's famous slides.

I stepped back and smiled in greeting. "How are you doing today, Jennifer? Did you enjoy your breakfast?"

"Delicious! Do you do fresh flowers with every meal?"

"Every one," I answered.

"I put the daisy in my book." She blushed. "It's something my mom used to do."

"To press them. I remember doing that," I said.

"It's fun. I do it all the time. Then, when I go to reread that particular book, I'll see it and remember that day. Speaking of which, it was gorgeous yesterday. I daresay I got a suntan!" She showed off a slightly pink, freckled arm.

I inspected it. "That looks more like a sunburn to me."

She laughed. "That's the best suntan I'll ever get. I need to wear a shirt today. I left my sunscreen back at the last hotel."

"Oh really? Come with me and I'll get you some. No one should have to wear extra clothing on a beautiful day like today."

At the desk, I informed Sierra and the receptionist rummaged in our guest closet for some sunscreen.

"If you have anything you need, just come to the desk. We'll take care of you." I said.

I would have continued my conversation with Jennifer, but just then Kristi came through the revolving door. Decked out in full police attire, she strode across the foyer with determined steps. Ryan Marshall followed behind, trying to make it appear like it wasn't an effort to keep up with his partner.

Clarissa immediately perked up at the sight of the male police officer. "Can I help you?" she asked in that cheerful tone of hers.

"I've got it," I said, stepping next to her. "What's up? What'd you discover?"

"Can we talk privately?" Kristi asked, her eyes darting over to where Jennifer stood. I excused myself from Jennifer and led the officers into my office.

The moment the door closed, Kristi shot off like a machine gun. "Mr. Dayton had definitely been staged in that bed. The coroner said there was livor mortis on the tops of his thighs which means he died face down. And a slight abrasion mark on the back of his head that indicated a contusion from when he was moved."

"Livor mortis?"

"It's the term for the way blood settles."

I thought about the vomit. "I wonder if he died in the bathroom?"

"Why do you guess that?" Kristi asked.

"Because I remember there was a pile of hair at the threshold. It could have gotten trapped and pulled out if he'd been dragged out of the bathroom."

"Well, whoever did it was careful to place him perfectly, even pulling the blankets up under his arms. I'm going to need a key to that room. We're putting it under a microscope. The forensics team is already on their way." She tucked her short hair around her ear and I wondered if she was considering my theory. She continued, "By the way, one of your cleaning employees wasn't too happy this morning."

"Who, Michelle?"

"Yeah. She had to come down and give her fingerprints so we can eliminate them."

"Do I need to go down?"

"Nope. We already have yours on file."

I looked up sharply. "I don't like the way you just said that."

She laughed. "Just give me the key, Maisie."

I passed it over and Kristi took it, still chuckling.

We headed back out and the two police officers walked over to the elevator.

I glanced at Clarissa and did a double take. "Girl, your mouth is hanging open. I think you might have actually drooled."

"Oh, sorry." She twisted a long curl around her finger. "But that man is yummy."

I chuckled and walked back into my office.

Line three was blinking on my phone. I sank into the chair and picked up.

"Oceanside hotel, Maisie Swenson, General Manager, speaking."

"Ah, Mrs. Swenson,"

I ignored the automatic missus added to my title. "Yes, how can I help you?"

"I am Dwayne Smith, Vincent Dayton's uncle." The man paused, waiting for my response.

Another relative? "I'm very sorry for what's happened," I said, leaning back in my chair.

"Yes. Yes. It's been quite a blow. At any rate, the police told me to come down and collect his belongings."

I closed my eyes at the stab at my temple. In all the time I'd spent at the hotel, I'd never had anything like this happen. Now two people wanted to collect Dayton's belongings?

"I see. Well, we've had someone come by to do just that. Unfortunately, the hotel requires proper identification, and the person went home to retrieve it. But I can get your number if that person falls through?"

"Someone else? Who else could there be? I'm his only living relative."

My eyes widened as a cold shock electrified my blood. "You're his only living relative?" I repeated, probably sounding very dull as I tried to process what he said.

"Yes, his parents passed years ago. And my nephew never married."

"He doesn't have a half-brother?"

"A half-brother?" The man scoffed. "No, Vincent was an only child."

I reached for the rubber band and made a face when I realized it was gone. I opened the drawer and searched for a paperclip to unbend as a substitute. But instead of that, my fingers found a pile of wet stuff. I jerked the drawer open to discover instant glue had somehow leaked from its container into a puddle. I stared at my fingertips in horror and immediately spread my fingers to avoid them touching.

Doing my best to maintain a professional tone in my voice, I continued. "I see. That does put a twist in this. I think the best thing for the hotel to do is to hand over Mr. Dayton's possessions to the police and have the next of kin pick them up from there."

I tried to scrape off the blob with a paperclip. Dismay hit me as the paperclip stuck to my fingertip. I waggled it in panic.

"Oh." The change in his tone was palpable. He exhaled heavily through his nose, causing a noisy whine.

After a few seconds of waiting for a response, I continued. "So, Mr. Smith, I can get you the number to our local police department." Gritting my teeth, I yanked off the clip. Holy mother— I bit back a scream.

"There is something else, something that needs great care not to become lost. An envelope. Nothing valuable in it but letters from my father when he was at war. Vincent liked to carry it with him for sentimental reasons. But I would like to have that back. If I could just swing by..."

The sting of my finger was forgotten at hearing the envelope in the safe referenced again. I highly doubted it carried nostalgic letters from some beloved father.

"I'm sorry, Mr. Smith. I'm afraid my decision stands. We will be compiling everything together to be picked up at the station. Let me give you the number. Do you have a pen?" I shook my fingers to dry the glue.

At his grunt, I quickly rattled off the Starke Springs police department number.

"Now, is there anything else I can help you with?" I tapped my fingers and nearly groaned as I realized my fingertips no longer felt sensation due to the hardened shell of glue. Lovely.

"I find you extremely unhelpful in this time of grief. I can scarcely believe you would take a chance that a family heirloom might be lost due to the bureaucracy of red tape rather than hand it over. You'll be hearing from my attorney."

This day was just getting better and better. "I completely understand. You need to do what you feel is best. It's in the hotel's best interest to have the police sort out who is an actual relative so that the letter doesn't go to an imposter."

At this point, I was speaking to dead air. He'd hung up.

Sighing, I returned the phone to the receiver and glanced at the safe. What was in that envelope?

CHAPTER 11

*J*sent a text to Kristi about yet another strange relative asking for Dayton's stuff. By lunch time I still hadn't heard back from Kristi. I had a feeling it would be awhile since she was searching the room. I couldn't imagine what she would find, and I jittered around all morning with nervous energy like lighting was about to strike.

And the air sure felt electrified.

But, I still hadn't heard anything by the time I headed back to my suite for the night. My day had been spent mostly on wrestling down my distraction so I could focus on administrative tasks. Julie had been happy to report the sheets were in and the crisis averted, and Mrs. Richardson did indeed get her free ticket to the show. I still needed to figure out what to do with the coffee pots and what I was going to say in the letter to Mr. Phillips.

Momma wasn't home when I walked in, probably out on one of her little errands. She didn't drive, but the senior center sent a bus every day. It was a common thing to see the white vehicle with the portrait of a happy elderly couple pasted across its side parked in front of the hotel.

Bingo lay under the table when I got myself a cup of tea. He looked at me with sorrowful eyes. I started to baby talk him when I noticed a few suspicious crumbs on his muzzle.

"What have you been into?" I asked suspiciously.

The dog arched an eyebrow at me before bouncing up the other as he looked away.

I watched him for a moment, but he was clearly ignoring me now. All signs that he'd gotten into something. I glanced around. There was nothing obvious in the kitchen. I took my tea into the living room, searching for evidence.

Hmm, nothing in here either.

I walked into my room and sat before my laptop. A few clicks brought up what I'd written so far.

Dear Mr. Phillips,

I groaned in rereading it. That was it. My creative writing skills hadn't exactly been flowing like honey lately. Thinking of my boss made me think of Mr. Phillips' brother, Jake.

The two brothers couldn't be more opposite, with Jake being generous and low-key compared to Mr. Phillips' tightly wound skinflint-ness. Jake and I had been dating the last few months. Honestly, our first few dates had been disasters, and I was more than surprised when Jake still texted me. We had grown closer over the last few weeks, and I smiled at the last text he'd sent me.—**Miss you lady. Dinner when I get back?**

As weird as it made things between my boss and me, and despite the bad dates, Jake and I had a lot of fun. He was easy to talk with and made me laugh, and I still got butterflies when we got together. He'd been away on business the last two weeks, and I couldn't wait for our dinner. The excitement to see him was definitely making it hard to craft a letter convincing his brother to spend a few thousand dollars improving something I'm sure Mr. Phillips thought was good enough.

I stared at the screen, trying to force the words to come. Gah! Maybe I should work on my novel instead.

I'd been writing a mystery for months. Like sixteen months. Taking a sip of tea, I opened up the file and scanned the predicament where I'd last abandoned Miranda, my amateur sleuth.

The guard dog circled the tree that Miranda had managed to scramble up into. A steady growl vibrated from the animal's throat, showing itself as a plume of fog in the cold air. The dog's lip curled, revealing an impressive set of sharp, white teeth. Miranda shivered and adjusted her grip on the branch.

Not bad. Not bad at all, I could feel my imagination start to fire. I stretched my fingers. I knew just where I wanted to go with this.

My cell phone vibrated on the table, causing ripples in my tea. *No!* My imagination screamed as my ideas started to dart away. *I can do this. I can remember them.* Quickly, I grabbed a piece of paper and jotted a few words down, hoping they'd remind me where to pick up.

Satisfied, I answered the phone. "Hello?"

"Okay, start at the beginning. You said an uncle and a brother both tried to get Dayton's personal effects?" As always, Kristi was direct and to the point.

"Yeah, and they both denied the existence of the other, saying they were Dayton's only living relative. I told them to contact the police department." I bit my lip, thinking about the envelope. "There's something else I forgot to tell you. Vincent Dayton left an envelope in the hotel safe under strict orders that if anything should happen to him, it would be delivered immediately to his attorney."

"Really?" Kristi said. "Now that's interesting."

"Yes. And the uncle and brother have both asked about the envelope."

Kristi sighed on the other end. "Sounds like I need to get a court order then to seize that envelope."

I breathed out in relief. I finally had an answer.

"As for that suite," Kristi continued. "We've finished our investigation. That place is cleaner than any I've ever seen."

"Cleaner? We'd barely started to clean when you called."

"Fingerprints. Except for yours and Michelle's, there wasn't another to be found."

"Even Mr. Dayton's?"

"Especially a lack of his. I'd say that's pretty weird, huh?"

"Very." I rubbed my arm. More than anything else, it proved there was foul play.

"So take that room out of the rotation schedule. It's definitely a crime scene."

"You got it." I wasn't worried about it getting reserved. Since Dayton hadn't checked out, it still showed up as unavailable.

"I'm taking his belongings into evidence and I'll come back with that court order for the stuff in the safe."

We said our goodbyes, and I hung up. The man wasn't paranoid after all. Someone had been in that room. But how?

Mike *must* have left. He had to be lying to me. And what about that envelope? That had to be the reason Dayton was killed.

I frowned harder. But if the killer was looking for the envelope, wouldn't the room have been ransacked? Everything was pretty much how I remembered it from the trip to his room the night before when he'd been very much alive. If his belongings had been searched through, then they were placed back in the same spot as they'd been in originally. Would a murderer be that conscientious?

Maybe if he was trying to make it look like it wasn't a murder.

Still, both the uncle and the brother knew about the envelope. But they clearly weren't working together. In fact, they denied each other.

I had to get hold of Mike again. I needed the truth. He must have left his post at some point, even if only for the bathroom. For some reason, maybe he was too scared to admit it.

I thought about calling him now. But he had just started his shift for the night, and I wanted him to be on his A game as much as possible. I didn't know if Mr. Stephenson would be returning, or if the uncle or some other random relative would show up, and I didn't want Mike rattled. My number one duty was to the hotel and the safety of the guests. I'd call him in the morning when his shift was over. Quickly, I scribbled a note to myself when I heard the front door to my suite open.

Momma called for me, "Maisie! Yoo-hoo! Are you here?"

I got up to greet her, bringing my mug with me. "How was your night, Momma? What'd you do?"

She was in the kitchen, man-handling what looked like a 16x20 canvas, which she propped against the fruit bowl, canvas side away from me. She also set down a bag with a red logo that looked suspiciously like our local craft store's name. Her penciled-on eyebrows raised as if daring me to ask about it.

I knew better than to take the bait and instead, rinsed the mug. Bingo slunk back under the table at the sight of Momma, reminding me of his guilty attitude earlier.

What was going on with that dog?

"Well, today we had a painting session. They had the supplies and help us with a design. And this is what I did." She spun it around. It was a colorful scene of a bird on a tree branch with spring flowers.

"Gorgeous!" I said, and I meant it.

"Thank you." She beamed. "I know just where I'm going to hang it." She lifted it with a grunt and carried it into her room.

I noticed she brought her bags of craft supplies with her. I shook my head and stacked my mug in the dishwasher.

Her door opened and then she screamed. I practically threw my back out racing around the corner to reach her.

"Momma! Are you all right?"

When I got to her room, one of her hands was on her hips, mouth open in indignation, and she was pointing.

"What is going on?" I wheezed, relieved to see she was okay.

"Just look.At.What.That.Dog.Did."

I turned to follow her finger. Her bedside table drawer was open and everything pulled out and onto the floor. On top of the pile was a box of vanilla wafer cookies. It had been torn open with bits of cardboard scattered everywhere.

Momma had been known to slip a cookie or two to the Basset Hound for a treat for years. It looked like the act had caught up with her.

"Oh, my gosh, how many cookies were in that box? Tell me it

wasn't new!" I spun to go search for the pudgy dog, certain the poor thing had bloat.

"About five," Momma called dryly after me. "I've been rationing them, and he's been mad at me. That's why the box is ripped open. Bingo couldn't get them out."

Bingo came around the corner then, eyes drooping sadly.

"Did you do it, you naughty pup? Did you eat all the treats?" Momma scolded. She eyed the dog and patted the bed. "Aww, come here and give me a kiss."

"Momma, you are so easy on him."

"I can't be mad at your brother! Do you see that face?"

It's not the first time she referred to the dog as my brother. I couldn't help but wonder what that meant. Excited to be forgiven, Bingo bounded over with his tail whipping back and forth. He climbed the stairs, huge toenails scrabbling and lay next to Momma with his head on her leg with a happy whuff.

"Well, if you're sure you're fine, I'm heading to bed."

Momma blew a kiss and I shut the door. I couldn't keep my eyes open any longer, and I had to be up early the next day. Who knew what was waiting for me tomorrow. After the craziness of today, I didn't even dare to even whisper that question out-loud.

But as I rested my head on the pillow something niggled at my mind. I clenched my eyes, making white stars shoot across the backs of my eyelids. The thought wasn't coming to me.

I dreamed that night. In every dream was a suitcase. Big ones, small ones. They lay around like open mouths waiting to devour anyone who walked by.

CHAPTER 12

The next morning, I woke up feeling like my eyes had been used as a preschooler's sandbox. I squinted into the darkness and rubbed at them, then stared at the black streak across the back of my hand.

It was then that I remembered that I hadn't washed my face before I'd gone to bed the night before. My eyes never were happy about me sleeping in mascara.

I stumbled to the bathroom. Brilliant light made me wince. I'd forgotten Momma had the maintenance man install LED bulbs in all the sockets. I glanced in the mirror and jumped. There was a certain reality of one's facial features that shouldn't be experienced illuminated like a microwave oven the first thing in the morning.

I groaned and began to splash water on my face. The crispness of it awakened me enough to go stumble into the shower.

Thirty minutes later, I was clean, conditioned, and my hair blown dry. I felt alive and ready to start the day.

A scratch at my door proved that Bingo realized I was awake. I opened it and he waddled in. Yep. Definitely too many snacks. He climbed into his favorite spot under my desk and heaved a contented sigh.

I applied some mascara, trying to remember what was on my to-do list this morning. Seeing my laptop open reminded me of my dream. Suitcases.

What was it about suitcases?

It came to me like a flash. That label on the handle had said Milan, not Madrid like Dayton had told me. And I'd wondered if it were a simple slip of the tongue.

Or had he been hiding something?

I yanked my chair out and sat, with Bingo grumbling that he had to scoot over to make room for my feet. I felt like I needed to look into these two cities. Call it a hunch, but whenever I got that gut feeling I paid attention to it.

Come on. Come on. I drummed my fingers on the desk as I

waited for my laptop to wake up, my foot dancing up and down to rub Bingo's neck. Finally, the search engine opened. I typed in Madrid in the engine, chewing the inside of my cheek, not at all sure of what I was looking for. A list popped up of travel sites, with a few news stories sprinkled among them.

I scrolled down the list. Nothing stood out to me.

I typed in Milan and waited for the results. A new list populated, showing the same things as before. Quickly, my eyes scanned the lines. Tour site. Population information. A fight broke out at a restaurant.

Wait. What was this?

Judge reprimands courthouse security.

The article was from a few days prior. I clicked the link to read.

Judge Corroley called out courthouse security, Austin Maricio for failing to guard evidence gathered against one of the mob bosses, Dario Torino. The diamonds, estimated in the millions, disappeared overnight. Judge Corroley was forced to drop charges against Mr. Torino in light of the missing evidence. Torino was accused of having a long reaching arm clear to NY with affiliations with third circuit judge Martin Davis.

There was a picture of the guard, taken from a security badge. He was a thin man with black-and-white hair and was clean-shaven. His hair was slicked back, accentuating a long nose, and a lined forehead.

Maricio has since disappeared. He was last seen at the courthouse with an unidentified man in his late fifties. Images from courthouse cameras give us this picture.

Below it was a fuzzy picture of two men of nearly indiscernible features. One was clean shaven—presumably Maricio although the black-and-white photo made it impossible for a positive identification—while the other man was dressed in a plain Oxford shirt. What stood out to me was how the other man stood, with his shoulders rolled forward and his hand on his head as if he were trying to slick back a comb-over.

Was it possible that was Vincent Dayton? I closed the laptop, feeling my forehead wrinkle. So who were those men coming in to look for the envelope, really?

My cell buzzed, cutting off my thoughts. "Hello?" I answered.

"Ms. Swenson?" It was Clarissa, and she sounded stressed.

"Yes. What's going on? Is everything okay?"

"Everything's fine. There's a gentleman here to speak with you."

"Okay. I'll be right down," I said, trying not to visualize another disaster awaiting for me.

"Wonderful. He's anxious to talk with you." Her normally bright voice grew muffled. "I've called Mike to come up as well."

My skin prickled at the mention of the hotel security. Something was up. "Understood. Can you have Mike escort the gentleman into my office and then wait there with him?" It sounded like trouble and I wanted it as far away as the guests as possible.

"Yes, ma'am."

"Thanks, Clarissa."

I scooted Bingo from my room and shut the bedroom door behind me. After a hurried greeting to Momma, I ran from the suite. My fingers itched for something to fiddle with. Who was down there waiting for me? And what had he done to make Clarissa already call for security?

As I WALKED down the hall, I fanned my shirt a bit to

conceal any nervous sweating. I wasn't sure of what I was about to see. People were leaving the hotel for their day's activities. I didn't want a ruckus to happen in their midst. Why did this all have to be happen when the hotel critic was here?

I heard him before I saw him.

Mr. Stephenson.

"Are you getting the manager here or not? You do have someone who runs this joint, don't you?" The man's offended voice echoed.

I walked briskly into the foyer to be faced with Mr. Stephenson scowling at Clarissa. It was a good thing Sierra wasn't working, or she'd be giving the attitude right back to him.

But, then again, seeing Clarissa, who was soft and sweet, cower from the man kind of made me wish Sierra *was* there to give it to him.

"Mr. Stephenson," I called out in a stern tone. "I'm right here. How can I help you?"

"Well, it's about time!" he snapped. "I've been waiting forever." He strode toward me, his loafer heels clicking against the floor. "Will this work for you?" He brandished his wallet, which had his driver's license in the plastic ID pocket.

I glanced at it. Mr. Vito Stephenson was his given name. Squeezing my hands into fists, I braced myself. It was time to give him the hard news.

"There seems to be a discrepancy on who Mr. Dayton's family members are."

The short man's face flushed, making his ruddy skin appear purple. He sputtered, as if out of words. "What?" he finally barked out. "Who's saying this?"

I swallowed hard. "Another family member called yesterday to claim Mr. Dayton's personal items."

"Another...?" Mr. Stephenson's mouth dropped in astonishment. He spun around to his bodyguards. "Are you hearing this?"

They solemnly nodded. Mr. Stephenson turned back to me and puffed out his chest. "Now listen here, missy."

"It's Ms. Swenson," I said.

"I don't care who you are. I'm Vincent Dayton's older brother. There ain't no one else. Just the two of us."

From the corner of my eye, I noticed another man walking up to us. He wore a three-piece navy-blue suit and silk tie. His salt-and-pepper hair, more black than white, was styled in a tall swoop. He had a trimmed beard that followed a strong jawline, and a beak-like nose that didn't detract from his subtle handsomeness.

"Ah, Ms. Swenson," the new man said when he realized he'd caught my attention. His eyes crinkled at the corners. "Finally, we meet."

CHAPTER 13

"Jf you could just give me one moment, sir," I said to the new person, holding my hand up. My mind was whirling. "Maybe wait just over there, and I'll be right with you." I pointed to an impressionist painting on the far wall.

The new man took a step back, dipping his chin in respect as he watched me.

Okay. Back to the first fire. "I'm sorry to have to tell you this. Mr. Stephenson, but the Starke Springs police department are the ones you need to be in contact with about Mr. Dayton's personal items. They'll probably require proof of your relationship with Mr. Dayton," I said.

"Proof! You keep asking for proof! I came back with what you asked for the first time!" Furiously, the short man shook the wallet at me. Then he seemed to try to control himself. He closed his eyes, his chest heaving as he took a deep breath. Clenching his teeth, he gritted out, "My brother died here. You are making it very difficult for me to move on. This is preposterous."

It was here the second man stepped forward again. "Ms. Swenson, it's vital that I talk with you. This man is an imposter."

The entire foyer seemed to be collectively holding their breath at the salt-and-pepper haired man's announcement. I could have heard a pin drop.

Mr. Stephenson slowly swiveled on one loafer until he faced his accuser. His face showed no emotion as he stared. But the threat was there. Unmistakeable.

The other man seemed unperturbed. Ignoring the shorter man, he thrust forward his hand to me. "Mr. Dayton has told me all about you." He smiled and his green eyes twinkled.

Oh no. Not another Dayton relative. They seem to be multiplying like mosquitos at sundown. I hardly knew what to do with the offered hand, with Mr. Stephenson fuming next to me. I gave it an uneasy shake, waiting to hear the story.

"I'm Devin Austin, Vincent Dayton's attorney." He released

me and began patting himself down. "Oh, yes. Let me get this." With that, he pulled out a leather wallet and flipped open to a Connecticut driver's license.

I leaned over and scrutinized it. *Hmmm, David Austin.* Five-foot-nine inches. Gray hair. Brown eyes. One hundred and sixty pounds. His smiling face stared out from the photograph.

I glanced up at him and he smiled again. His hand stroked his beard and explained. "I go by my middle name. After my grandfather."

"You're kidding me. Are you just going to let this guy waltz in here and schmooze you? He's the imposter!" Mr. Stephenson yelled.

I was hardly paying attention to Stephenson's protests, I was staring so hard at Mr. Austin. Where had I seen him before?

The lawyer didn't bat an eye at the short man pontificating before him. He reached into his jacket and retrieved a folded document. "I know Mr. Dayton has something in your safe. It was meant to go to me in the unexpected event of his death. Sadly, that event seems to have happened. I have verification right here." He handed over the document.

Mr. Stephenson pushed between me and the lawyer. "What in the world? Are you just going to let this bozo call me, Vincent's only flesh and blood, an imposter? What kind of hotel manager are you, anyway? You couldn't manage to keep flies off a picnic basket." He flourished his open wallet in my face again. "Isn't this what you were asking for?"

I stepped back with the papers, my head swiveling between the two of them like I was at a tennis match.

"You're a liar," Mr. Austin said mildly. And then to me, "Go ahead and read it. It's all there."

I opened up the paper and scanned it. It was signed and notarized a few days prior, decreeing that Mr. Dayton bequeathed all of his effects, including a document to be found in the hotel safe, to his attorney, Devin Austin, in the event of his death during his travels.

Mr. Stephenson's eyes bobbed between the paper and my face. "What is it? What does it say?" he demanded.

I contemplated my next step. Legally, this meant I needed to pass the suitcase over, and more importantly, the envelope. But I knew that Kristi was on her way with a search warrant.

This document suddenly made things very complicated.

And why did he look so darn familiar to me?

I decided to cut to the chase. "Mr. Stephenson. Mr. Austin. We've released all of Mr. Dayton's personal items to the Starke Springs police department. I can get you the number if you would like."

"And the envelope?" Mr. Austin asked, his eyes narrowing. Mr. Stephenson watched for my reaction too.

I hesitated. I didn't want to tell them it was still in the safe. Heaven only knew what might happen then.

"I'm sorry, both of you. There's really nothing more I can do. You will both have to contact the police for further information. This investigation is in their hands now."

"Investigation! What investigation? Are you saying he was murdered?" Dayton's purported half-brother shouted.

My grip on my professionalism slipped, and my hand flapped to cover my eyes. *Good one, Maisie.* "No. But the police are always involved whenever someone passes away at the hotel. This really is out of the hotel's control."

"I seriously doubt you had any, to begin with." Mr. Stephenson clenched his fists. "I'm digging into this, and if I find out the hotel was negligent in any way"—his finger jerked up to point in my face—"I'm coming after you personally, missy."

Mr. Austin watched mildly as Mr. Stephenson whirled around and stomped out the door. The short man's two bodyguards glowered at me in disapproval, before following their boss.

"I'm sorry. The same goes for you too," I reaffirmed to the lawyer.

Mr. Austin straightened his jacket, giving me a slow nod, and slowly trailed after them.

My insides shook as I watched them leave. Several of the hotel guests stared from the sidelines. I had to address them.

"Not to worry, folks. Everything is okay. Please, go about your day and enjoy the beautiful sunshine," I said with a cheeriness I definitely didn't feel.

"You okay?" Clarissa appeared next to me.

I forced myself to smile. "I'm fine. That was very strange. I feel for whoever has to deal with him in the future. Now, how are you?"

"Oh, man. That short guy was…interesting. I really didn't know what I was going to do when he said he was going to tear the place apart."

"He said that?" I asked.

"Yeah. With his bare hands, he said, looking for his brother's stuff."

At that moment, Mike came down the hall.

"Thanks for showing up in the nick of time," Clarissa said sarcastically.

"What? Where is he? What do you want me to do?" he asked, looking around for trouble.

"We wanted you here about fifteen minutes ago," Clarissa said with her arms crossed.

"I'm sorry." He shrugged, his huge shoulders making his uniform go tight across his chest. "I had to make a phone call. That officer had some questions for me."

"Officer Bentley?" I asked.

"Yeah, that's the one. Your friend."

"And what did she want?"

His brow wrinkled. He rubbed the back of his neck, suddenly appearing unsure. "Nothing. Just asked over and over if I'd heard anything the night you left me to guard Mr. Dayton's room. If I'd left my post. That sort of thing."

"And did you? Did you leave your post?"

"Absolutely not!" Defensiveness lifted his volume. "Not until I called you in the morning and got permission."

"Not even," I hesitated, "for a bathroom break or to grab something to eat?"

He blinked as if he'd been caught. "Listen, even then I got someone to cover it."

137

So he *did* leave. "Who covered it?"

"I called one of the housekeepers to come up. Michelle, I think it was."

I frowned, thinking of the housekeeper with the long braid. Why hadn't she mentioned it to me when we were in the room?

I nodded. "All right. Thank you. Now I'd like you to go out to the parking lot and make sure everything is quiet out there." With the lawyer outside with Mr. Stephenson, I didn't want there to be any trouble.

"You got it. Anything specific I should be watching for?" Mike asked.

"Mr. Dayton's so-called brother was just here, threatening to make trouble. And then Dayton's lawyer. They both recently left." I glanced at the door. "I'm not entirely sure they won't be back. I need to get hold of Kristi."

"Well, like I said, I just got off the phone with her. So give her phone a try," Mike pointed.

"Thanks, Mike. Before you leave, please update the rest of your team. Mr. Stephenson is not allowed back on hotel property."

He nodded, and I turned to head back to my office. My gaze landed on someone in the shadows.

Mrs. Richardson.

I shivered, suddenly wondering at her constant appearance at the worst possible times. She shook her head at me in disapproval. I hesitated and started walking toward her. At my action, she turned and disappeared down the hallway toward the elevator.

My heart did a double beat as I imagined what review she was going to leave the Oceanside.

Pull it together, girl. You still have a dead body to deal with, and if it leaks that he was murdered, that press will be worse.

My thoughts went to Kristi. *Need you to hurry with that search warrant, lady. Time's running out.*

CHAPTER 14

$\mathcal{I}$ walked into the office, needing a moment to myself to sort out what just happened and to figure out a game plan. It was then that I realized I was still holding the paperwork that Mr. Austin had given me.

I stared at the safe. What if the papers had the evidence from the trial? Did it hold diamonds? I texted Kristi. Even though Mike had said he'd just gotten off the phone with her, I hesitated to call. I never knew if she was in a stakeout or I might be putting her life in danger, even though I knew she turned her phone off during those times.

—Lawyer showed up with official papers to pick up Dayton's envelope. What do I do?

I guess she really was available because she texted right back.

—Stall him. On my way to the judge right now.

Stall him. Well telling him to visit the police department seemed to work for now, but what if Austin came back? And he would since I had his paperwork. In fact, he'd probably be back any minute. I rubbed my temples and stared desperately around my office as if I could find a way to stall him sitting on the desk or file cabinet.

Nothing. My fingers went to my lanyard where I kept the main hotel pass-key, along with the key to the safe. *That's right!* It took two keys to open the safe. Sierra had one, and Steve the other. Perfect. I'd tell Mr. Austin that the person with the other key wasn't in yet.

It wasn't the greatest resolution because it made the hotel look incompetent. But beggars couldn't be choosers, and at least I'd come up with an excuse.

I squared my shoulders, practicing the wording in my head. *So sorry, Mr—*

My office phone rang from the front desk.

"Hello?" I answered.

"Ms. Swenson?" It was Clarissa. "Mrs. Richardson is on line four. She's saying that no one answered her phone call to the front desk, but I promise you I didn't miss it."

"Hm, well maybe when that drama with Mr. Stephenson happened."

"I stayed by the phone the whole time."

I slowly exhaled. "Is she checking out today?"

I could hear Clarissa typing and then she said. "Yes! Check out at noon."

Okay, I only have a few more hours to fix this. "All right, thank you. I'll handle it. Could you please send a memo to Julie to have her pack up Mr. Dayton's belongings?"

I hung up and thought about that. Mrs. Richardson couldn't have called when Mr. Stephenson was at the hotel. I'd just seen her there in the lobby.

I clicked the button to answer line four. "Hello, Mrs. Richardson. How can I help you this morning?"

"Ms. Swenson. My coffee decanter is missing. After no one answered my call for room service, I finally took it upon myself to go downstairs to get help. But after watching the debacle from this morning, I can well understand why this hotel is run so shoddily. This hotel has more drama than any soap opera I've ever seen."

I eased out a deep sigh. Immediately, thoughts of the hotel hack of ramen noodles cooking in the carafe came to my mind. Housekeeping must not have replaced her coffee pot.

"I'm so sorry, Mrs. Richardson. I'll have someone bring you up a fresh cup of coffee. Can I offer you something for breakfast?"

"This is ridiculous!" she spat out in answer.

"I'll take care of everything. Again, I'm so sorry."

"And that ticket you sent me to the comedy show?" A sniff came through the phone's receiver, and then her plaintive voice complained. "Five rows back. Hardly what I call front row seats."

Just then, my office door was nudged open. Mr. Austin poked his head around the corner. My stomach sank. Why had Sierra let him back here? I waved at the lawyer to leave. Ignoring me, he edged in further and then turned to face the safe.

My temple throbbed with pain. "I see. Well, I hope you were able to enjoy the comedy show all the same."

Mr. Austin tested the handle. I needed to get off the phone.

"Just be sure to send my coffee. And a nice plate of eggs and bacon would be nice. But I want them sunny-side up. Not cooked to disks like yesterday!"

"Absolutely. Right away," I said.

With a final harrumph, she hung up.

I immediately stood angrily. "Mr. Austin, it's completely inappropriate for you to come into my office without knocking."

"Sorry?" he said, turning to face me with a million watt smile. "I did knock, but you must not have heard. The knocking is what opened your door. I thought I'd wait quietly until you were finished."

"Would you like someone to go into your office uninvited when you were on the phone?"

His smile froze. Tipping his chin, he said, "Ah, but my conversations are a protected privilege. Hardly what I'd call what you do here, running coffee up to disgruntled guests."

I resisted the urge to roll my eyes. "Here is your document." I pushed it forward across the desk.

"Yes." He reached for it, and his fingertips tapped the paper in any annoying staccato. "Legally, what's Mr. Dayton's property in that safe is mine. I don't believe the police have possession of it yet. I'm an attorney, so I understand that takes time to get the proper paperwork."

I ignored his comment. "I'm sorry to tell you that the safe is opened with two keys. The person with the other key isn't here. I'll be happy to call you when she shows up."

He sat on the edge of my desk. "Ah, my little nightingale. What are you doing?"

"Excuse me?" I crossed my arms.

He gave me a patient smile. "The person with the other key. Sierra's her name, isn't that correct? I just walked into the hotel with her. We had a lovely chat and apparently, she's here starting her shift. What game are you playing at, Maisie?"

CHAPTER 15

The hair on the back of my neck rose. He knew my given name. And he knew who Sierra was.

I needed to get him out of my office right now. I grabbed the phone and yelled, before anyone even answered, "Call Security." He didn't need to know if I was actually talking with someone.

"Ms. Swenson?" Sierra answered.

"Security!" I shouted again.

Mr. Austin flinched like my word was a whip. He gathered his paper and tucked it into his coat.

"You'll be hearing from me very soon," he warned.

"Yeah, yeah, I know the drill. All of you people connected

with Mr. Dayton sound the same," I said.

Steve burst through the door. He immediately eyed Mr. Austin and narrowed his eyes. "Ms. Swenson?"

"Get him out," I said.

Steve made a move as if to grab the lawyer's arm. Austin jerked his arm away. "I don't need your help."

Steve stepped back from the door and Austin walked through. The lawyer didn't look at me again. I didn't know if I should be relieved or if that was a bad sign.

A second later, Sierra showed up. "I am so sorry. He came back here when I was taking a reservation for a convention." Subconsciously, she pulled at the half-sleeve that partially covered a long red scar. It was rare that I saw Sierra appear insecure.

"He said you guys chatted," I said.

"Yeah. We had a moment at the revolving door where I didn't know if he was going to go first or not. He waved me forward and then squeezed in with me. It was awkward, but he seemed friendly enough."

I sank back in my chair wearily. "It's fine. Those things happen." I glanced at the clock. Almost ten. "You know, I'm getting out of here until Kristi arrives. I'll be out checking on staff. If you need me, call."

She nodded and left the office. I followed, locking the door behind me.

Steve strode back across the foyer from the front door. "He's gone, boss."

"Thanks, Steve. Keep me posted."

I headed home to my suite. I needed a reboot and maybe some food. Actually, I knew exactly what I was looking for. Even at thirty-five, I needed my mom.

I opened the door and slipped off the responsibility and, for a few moments, became my mother's little girl.

"Maisie? Has that kerfuffle settled down?" Momma called from the kitchen.

I smiled at the sound of her voice and undid the strap of my shoes. Scents of what smelled suspiciously of homemade waffles pulled me down the hall.

"How do you know it's me?" I asked.

She was at the table, crossword puzzle before her, and glanced at me from over the tops of her glasses. "And just who else would be coming through the door?"

I was disappointed not to see any waffles. My stomach growled. "I don't know. An axe murderer?"

I thought she might make fun of my crazy imagination, but

instead, she pursed her lips. It was then that I remembered her new obsession with watching the crime channel.

"You know, you're right. I should find myself a weapon, just in case." She got up and rifled through the utensil jar. With a shout of triumph, she seized the meat tenderizer.

"What would you do with that, Momma?"

"Well, bounce it off of some idiot's skull, that's what." She tested it by giving it a few swings.

"Momma, sometimes you scare me."

She waved a hand. Her nail polish was perfect—mauve pink —like it always was. "Pish. Now, what's going on? You ran out of here like a rabbit in springtime, and now you're back before lunch time. And you missed breakfast."

"I'm starving," I admitted, opening the fridge. Forty-seven butter containers stared back at me, containing who knew what kinds of leftovers.

"I believe it. You've been so busy lately, you haven't been taking care of yourself."

And, just like that, I completed my transformation from hotel manager of one of the most elite hotels to a school kid, at least in Momma's eyes. I grabbed a container and popped the lid to peek inside. Macaroni and cheese. *Works for me.*

"You know what's strange?" I asked, grabbing a plate from the cupboard. I dumped the noodles on to it.

"Maisie, don't mumble. What's strange?"

I wasn't mumbling, but Momma would never admit to a hearing loss. "What's strange," I repeated, "Is that the tag on his suitcase didn't match the country he said he was returning from."

"He? Who's he? That crazy guy who went and died on us?"

"Yeah. Mr. Dayton. When he checked in, he said he was returning from Spain. But his luggage tag said Milan."

"Italy, huh?" She frowned as she watched me. "Maisie, don't eat that. I've got something better for you." She moved over to the fridge and poked about for a second. A second later, she came out with a plastic-wrapped plate of quiche. This she stuck in the microwave and then rummaged through the cupboard and brought out "the special mug." It was thick and black with a deer's profile on it. I smiled when I saw it. I'd given it to my dad years ago for Father's day.

"What are you thinking, Maisie?" Momma asked.

"Thinking about dad. I miss him." I shot a glance at Momma. Usually, I was more careful about that, not wanting to upset her.

She did look a little misty-eyed. Blinking hard, she set the mug down.

I hurried over and gave her a hug. "I'm sorry. I didn't mean to make you sad."

She patted my hand. "I miss him, too. He was a good man. You know, the good Lord sets the exact number of steps to every man." She sighed. "That's why I never took up jogging."

Her unexpected remark caused a chuckle to shoot out of me, followed by a snort as I tried to cut it off.

"Maisie, don't snort. It isn't ladylike. And I'm serious. You won't catch me wasting my steps like that." With that, she filled the mug with coffee and carried it to the table. "Now, come sit."

AFTER I ATE, I dug out my sandals from the closet and took Bingo for a walk to the hotel's pet park. The sun was bright overhead, and I could hear splashing and laughter from the pool. As the days got longer, so did the activity around the hotel.

Mrs. Richardson popped in my mind and anxiety shot

through me. I pulled out my phone to send Ruby a text. —**AHHH!**

My message must have sent her a panic-ridden brain bullet because she sent me back —**Quit worrying. It's going to be okay.**

I smiled at her text, but was it going to be okay? I glanced over at the dog and took a deep breath. Bingo sat in a patch of sunlight and panted happily before turning to sniff the air. That dog was the picture of contentment. Purposely, I rolled my neck and lowered my shoulders. *Relax. Be present in the moment.*

Dayton's difference between Milan and Madrid drove in like a battering ram. And what about that crazy article I'd read earlier? Did Dayton have a slip of the tongue? Was he somehow involved in that theft? It was hard to imagine him being a jewelry thief at his age.

I thought about all these relatives sprouting out of the wood-work. A half-brother, the uncle, and now a lawyer. And why hadn't Kristi gotten back to me about her search warrant? What was taking her so long?

Bingo had found a flower to pounce on. I hated to disturb him, but I had to do some more digging into all of this. It was driving me crazy. I clucked my tongue and led him back to the suite.

BACK IN MY OFFICE, I logged into the hotel's reservation system, just to see if I could find a clue where Mr. Dayton arrived from. Sometimes the guests asked for shuttle service from the airport, which meant we sent a driver to meet them at the arrival gate. Ahh. There it was, room 360. Reservation was made two weeks prior by D. R. Austin. I already knew the lawyer had made Dayton's reservation. I scrolled further to read the instruction sheet of guest preferences.

There *was* concierge service requested for pick up at gate eighteen. I needed to look that up to see what flights used that gate throughout that day.

I was about to log out when my gaze landed on the reservation for room 359. It'd been made under the name John Doe— not too unusual in the hotel business— and they'd reserved the suite for a week. The odd part was that they never showed up. They didn't even give a cancellation phone call, especially since they'd been billed for 70% of the room fee. It was in the reservation that the room would only be held until noon the next day, with the first night billed to the reserving guest regardless of whether they checked in or not.

Something about that was making my feelers lift. I clicked on the billing for room 359. There was a foreign transaction fee. I clicked the charge and dug into the file deeper.

The name on the card was D. R. Austin.

A chill ran down my back. I returned to the main screen and sat there frozen.

Could there be some kind of mistake? A fluke in the system? I clicked on room 359 now, which I'd hastily given to Mrs. Richardson. Quickly, I scrolled to the billing. There it was again. D. R. Austin. Something was seriously wrong here. The billing system had to be glitching.

My phone buzzed, making me jump. Kristi's no-nonsense voice came through the speaker. "Okay, lady. I've got the warrant. I'll be down to get the letter and the rest of Dayton's items."

"Something weird is going on here," I mumbled back, distracted.

"What? I can't hear you. What's the matter?"

"Something is weird with our billing system. It looks like Dayton's attorney also paid for Mrs. Richardson's room." I rubbed my neck, trying to figure it out. Finally, I concluded, "It's probably nothing. Somehow when the room got transferred, the name that didn't get erased. But I need to get a hold of the billing department to find out for sure what's going on."

"What made you look at all?"

"I wanted to know if the hotel picked Dayton up from the airport so I could figure out what country he was returning from."

"Why were you doing that?"

"His tag on his luggage didn't match where he said he was coming from."

"Did you find anything?"

"Not really. Just this weird billing issue." I bit the pad of my index finger, where a remnant of super glue remained.

"Well, did it occur to you that the tag might be from another trip?"

"Oh." I suddenly felt like an idiot. Had I built this whole case up on nothing?

"Leave the suitcase at the front desk and I'll pick it up, along with the stuff from the safe. We'll get this sorted out soon enough."

"Got it." My confidence buoyed since we were about to get some real answers. "I can't wait to find out what's inside that envelope."

"Ahem. Strictly police business, Maisie."

"What? I can't even know?" I was shocked.

She laughed. "We'll see. But only if it won't compromise my investigation."

Well, that was at least something.

"And you're done with the room? I can get it cleaned?"

"Not yet. Give me another twenty-four hours just in case something comes up."

"Maybe with the envelope," I hinted.

"Maybe."

"Any word from the coroner?"

"Not yet." With that, she hung up.

There was some relief in keeping Mr. Dayton's room off the roster. It was a popular suite, with its huge balcony, soaking tub and stone-inlaid shower with a waterfall. I knew it would have already been reserved tonight.

The thought of that room being filled with guests right after a murder filled me with unease. Maybe I'd see about keeping it off for a few days, just out of respect.

But respect for who? *Maisie, you're being silly, Get up there and make sure you have everything packed.*

I found a pair of gloves from a box in the supply office and walked to the elevator.

As I boarded, I shivered as I remembered Dayton's eyes when he questioned me about his room being haunted.

And what did the facts show? He died with a guard outside his room. We know that he was murdered because the settling pattern showed he had died face down.

What about that brandy bottle and cup? Where were they now?

There had been two wine bottles. But I just realized there'd been no wine glass either. Did Dayton just drink it from the bottle? Both bottles?

Anything was possible, I supposed.

Up at the suite, I used my pass-key and entered. The room smelled slightly of stale cigar smoke. I'm going to be honest, it was a little creepy being in there alone. Dayton had thought his room had been haunted. What had happened leading up to his death that had made him think that way?

I walked over to the couch and saw a t-shirt I'd missed earlier crammed into the crack. I pulled on the gloves and pulled it out. There was a sock on the side of the couch, and another near the window. Carefully, I searched for anything I'd missed and brought them to the suitcase and stuffed them inside.

Finally, everything was packed. My hands were sweating,

and I tugged off a glove. It tore at my wrist as I pulled. *What a cheap piece of crap. We really have to do better for our housekeeping.*

I stared at the green shred, and my brain sparked, trying to remind me of something. But just as I almost had it, it disappeared.

I walked back to the bathroom to see if I missed something. The ironing board in the closet alcove was still out just as before. No clothing here. I ran my hand down its surface, trying to figure out what Dayton had been thinking. Why had he pulled it down? Was he getting ready to iron that night? It seemed improbable, given the state of his wardrobe. But drunk people do strange things.

There were a few tiny white crumbs on it. I examined one. Just seemed like a chalky bit of the drywall. Maybe they were from the wall cubby from when he'd lowered the board.

Might as well put it away. I kicked in the front leg of the ironing board and pushed it back up into the wall. It locked into place with a solid click.

A whiff of something indescribable came from the bathroom, immediately bringing to my mind the memory of me donning rubber gloves. Those poor housekeepers and what they had to clean.

Wait a minute. Didn't Mike find a piece of a glove in here the night Dayton called me up? Obviously, the same thing happened to one of the housekeepers that happened to me.

I forgot it was still in my jacket pocket back in my room. I remember the latex had looked shredded, as if the glove had gotten pinched, and the wearer jerked away.

Mike said he'd found it on the floor of this closet. Kind of a weird place for it to be.

I studied the length of the ironing board and then up the wall to the ceiling tiles above. A shiver ran through my veins. One looked like it was missing a chunk from the corner. Had it been moved? Did those white crumbles come from the ceiling tile?

I snapped a picture of the tile and sent it to Kristi.

She texted back. **—What is this?**

I licked my lip. I wasn't sure. Not at all. She made fun of half my ideas, and I probably deserved it. After all, I had no clue what was beyond the ceiling tile. Probably just empty space.

But my gut told me this was it. Someone had moved that tile and pushed the ironing board down to have something to climb on. Maybe when Dayton woke up, the person escaped back through and tore his glove in the process of replacing the tile.

—I think I found out how they got into the room.

CHAPTER 16

A rustling at the suite's door made me nearly drop the phone. I jerked around and stared across the main room.

The handle turned slowly. My heart hammered against my ribs. Every muscle in my body tensed to make my getaway. But escape to where? I searched for a hiding spot, even momentarily considering hiding behind the sliding glass door curtain.

The door opened and a squeaking trolley pushed through. Our head housekeeper's eyes widened when she caught mine.

"Ms. Swenson?" Julie asked, a bit breathless.

Relief flooded through me, leaving me feeling boneless. I

grabbed onto the doorframe for balanced and took a few deep breaths.

"Julie! You scared me! What are you doing here?"

"You scared me too, boss," she said solemnly before closing the door. She wheeled the cart half-way into the room. "I got a note to pack up his things. What are you doing?"

"Oh, I forgot I'd sent that memo. The officer said she's on her way so I came in to make sure everything was ready." I suddenly felt miserable. "It haunts me that I'd talked to Dayton just hours before he was murdered. I'm the one who dismissed his fears."

"Aww, Ms. Swenson. You put a guard outside his door, so you didn't dismiss his fears. And we all thought he was a little special."

I could barely nod through the flood of guilt. I knew he hadn't seen a ghost but a real person. And I thought I could prove it. "Julie, you don't suppose.... How good are you at climbing?"

She looked at me like I was a few crayons short of a box. "Climbing? I haven't climbed anything since I was nine-years-old and fell out of my grandpa's apple tree."

I grunted in response. I guess it was going to be up to me then. "I think I know how they got in."

"They? Who?"

"The murderer. Come help me. And bring a pair of gloves."

I could hear Julie muttering under her breath as she rummaged for the gloves, but she had a noncommittal expression as she approached me. I pulled them on with a snap and led her to the closet.

"Just give me a hand," I said, as I pulled down the ironing board.

"Ms. Swenson, what on earth? Are you going to iron? Are you feeling okay?"

"I'm fine. Help me up."

Steadying myself, with one hand braced against the ironing board and the other on her shoulder, I climbed up. Metal groaned. The board wasn't designed to hold this much weight and wobbled a bit. Adrenaline shot through my nerves like white fire. I nearly fell, but, after flapping my arms, caught my balance.

Julie watched me with her lips puckered into a worried frown. After I felt somewhat secure, I flexed my fingers and then carefully pushed up on the ceiling tile.

Dust sifted as it moved. I shoved it to one side. Hot air filtered down like I'd opened a woodstove. I couldn't see past the metal lip of the opening into the blackness.

"Hold me steady, please," I commanded and reached for the far wall. With my other hand, I got out my phone and switched on the flashlight. Then, carefully, I rose on my toes.

Julie held me around the knees, muttering with a new fury.

Balancing against the ceiling opening, I was able to peep over the opening. I carefully guided the beam of light. My hands were sweaty, and I could just picture dropping the phone. There were marks in the dust like something had traveled through, and up ahead, the light glinted off of an object, but it was too far to make out what it was. I flipped the camera on and snapped, hoping the camera would focus on the object.

"Okay, I'm coming down," I warned and settled back to my heels. With one hand still against the wall, I studied the picture.

It was a coffee decanter.

What in the world? Was it the one from next door?

I stood on my toes again and peeked over the edge. Without the flashlight, I could see it was dark, but not the pitch black I'd imagined. The opening appeared to be a metal conduit of some kind. An outline of a rectangle, made of light, leaked ahead about thirty feet.

Right above Mrs. Richardson's suite.

Using my fingers, I tested the conduit's floor for strength. "I'm not sure if this could hold a person's weight."

"What?" Julie called from below.

I ducked my head to glance at her. "I said, I'm not sure if the tunnel could support a human. But maybe."

Sliding my hand on the wall for balance, I climbed down. Julie watched with her hands out like she'd catch me if I fell.

I studied the picture again, this time zooming in. What was the coffee decanter doing up there? And there appeared to be garbage stacked behind the carafe.

With a sigh, I sent the picture to Kristi.

"So, what do we do now, boss? Just pack things up?" Julie's forehead wrinkled.

"I'm not sure," I said. And I really wasn't. With this discovery, I figured the police would want to be back to examine it.

"Who do you think was up there?" Julie asked, her hands on her hip, staring at the black hole. "You don't think Mrs. Richardson...." She left the thought unfinished.

That crabby woman? Really, the near-perfect stereotype of every critic I'd ever met.

But was she really a mastermind behind this plan?

I rubbed my arm as goosebumps rose on it. I realized that whenever I'd seen Mr. Dayton, I'd seen Mrs. Richardson at the same time. And when Mr. Stephenson, the half-brother came by, she was there watching.

Was she the killer?

I rang the front desk.

"Oceanside hotel, Sierra speaking. How may I help you today?"

"Sierra! Has Mrs. Richardson checked out yet?"

"I—I don't believe so." Her voice faltered. "Are you okay?"

There was still time.

"I'm fine. Let me know if you see her. If she tries to check out, stall her!"

"Absolutely, I will." The confidence was back and her words crisp.

I hung up and started to text Kristi again. She'd just returned one to me. —**What's going on?**

—**Kristi, I know who the murderer is. Mrs. Richardson. Her room is connected to this one by the conduit. What do you want me to do?**

There were bubbles as Kristi typed her reply. I waited impatiently. I nearly shrieked when the phone rang, instead.

"Maisie Swenson, just what are you up to?" Kristi demanded.

I lowered my voice. I didn't want even a hint of a chance that Mrs. Richardson could hear me. "The ironing board was down. I found pieces of ceiling tile, and earlier Mike found a piece of a rubber glove. I climbed up there and there's ductwork that goes right over Mrs. Richardson's room."

"Yeah." Kristi's voice was infused with extra patience, which told me she was feeling anything but that.

"Well, above her crawl space was a bunch of garbage, including the coffee pot she was complaining was missing earlier."

The phone was silent for two beats. Then, "She complained her coffee pot went missing?"

I groaned. Seriously? With all those details *that's* what she picked up on? "You're not listening—"

"No. I hear you. You think she crawled through and killed him. But I'm curious why she'd complain the pot was missing. And what was her motive, anyway?"

"I don't know?" I was feeling panicked. Kristi better help me. "But what about that weird glitch that showed the same person paying for both rooms?"

"But that was the lawyer, right?"

I frowned. "Yes, I guess so."

"Don't worry. That's enough for probable doubt for me to at least question her. I'm coming down now."

"Well hurry, because she's about to check out."

"Sirens on," she said and hung up.

CHAPTER 17

*N*ext door, I heard rustling and then a thump. Julie and I looked at each other.

"Only ten more minutes to check out, Ms. Swenson," Julie whispered.

I glanced at my watch. Kristi was never going to get here in time. Panic made me feel like everything was moving a million miles an hour. How was I supposed to keep Mrs. Richardson here, and not suspicious, until Kristi arrived?

Was I strong enough to be able to restrain Mrs. Richardson if need be? I pictured the wrestling match. That would never work. I could barely control Bingo when he was after a grasshopper.

I knew what I could do. Quickly, I called Sierra. That girl had a chip on her shoulder the size of a hubcap, and she wasn't afraid to use it to whack some sense into a person. Luckily, through the time we've spent together, I've finally been able to earn her trust. But she was prickly when we'd first met, and I'd never forgotten that.

Turns out, sometimes being defensive is a good thing.

"How are things going down there?" I asked.

"Calm. Cool. Quiet," she answered.

"Any chance Clarissa can cover for you and you can run up here? I need some backup."

She didn't even question me. "You got it."

We hung up, and I glanced at Julie. "Okay, I need you to guard the elevator. Got that?"

"Guard?" She took a step back like there was a snake in her path.

I bit my lip. Julie was the antithesis of defensive. Every part of the short woman screamed soft and kind. "If Mrs. Richardson comes, try not to let her on the elevator. Delay and block the door, maybe with the cart. Act like the wheel is broken."

Julie nodded, and with a fierce determination I'd never before seen in the woman, pushed her cart out into the hall. She jutted her chin and marched down the hall, cart wheel squeaking.

I rang up Steve. "I need you to keep an eye out for Mrs. Richardson. You're going to need to be as persuasive as you can, but we can't let her leave."

"What's going on? We've been waiting all day for her to leave. Now you want to keep her?"

"It's complicated, but she may have something to do with Mr. Dayton's murder. The police are on their way."

He eased a whistle through his teeth. "Let me guess, she doesn't know you're on to her."

"You got it."

"Who's going to help *you*?" His lack of confidence in my ability was unsettling.

"Sierra is on her way."

"Oh, good." His voice ballooned with enthusiasm. "She'll sort her out."

"I can do it, too, Steve," I said, more defensive than I meant.

"Oh. Yeah. I know that."

I hate when my employees lie to me. "You just make sure she

doesn't leave the building," I snapped. At his confirmation, I said goodbye and hung up.

Okay. Just need to wait for Sierra to show up. Plus I needed a cover story for when I spoke with Mrs. Richardson. A good one.

I was pondering what to say when there was a knock at the door. A peek through the peephole showed Sierra, face flushed, hair back in a ponytail and earrings off.

I opened the door and pulled her in.

"Where is she? What do you want me to do?" Sierra's eyes darted around looking for the opponent.

"Shh, it's Mrs. Richardson." I hesitated, my fingers searching my wrist for the rubber band I normally kept there. Were my suspicions correct, or was I jumping to conclusions? "I think she may have had something to do with Mr. Dayton's murder. The police are on their way. But given how close checkout is, I was worried she'd leave before they got here."

"Exactly how did you come to this conclusion?" she asked, her eyes narrowing. She crossed her arms and stared.

"Wh—I, uh." Suddenly I felt foolish. Still, I pushed on with my data. "Mr. Dayton said someone woke him up, right? That first night. Well, Mrs. Richardson was in *this* room. She crawled through the conduit overhead. In fact, I remember

Mr. Dayton said he'd been woken up by a party going on upstairs. That was *her*. And whenever I had to go to the room, or there was police activity, she was there. And her coffee pot was up in the ceiling."

Sierra glanced at the ceiling. "I feel like I'm missing something." Her dry tone was unmistakable. She thought I was losing it.

"No. Wait!" I held my hand up as if I could physically keep her from jumping to conclusions. "The ironing board was down and—"

Her eyes narrowed further.

"Sierra, just give me a second. The ironing board was down and the ceiling tile in the closet moved. I checked up there and it connects to a crawl space that runs right past Mrs. Richardson's suite. Her missing carafe that she'd complained to me about earlier was up there."

The receptionist arched an eyebrow, her eyes glued to the ceiling. "Why would she want to kill Dayton?"

I shrugged, impatient at the small details. "It's complicated. It has to do with something I think he stole from a courthouse in Milan."

Now both of her eyebrows raised. "Why would she complain about a missing coffee pot if she's the one who put it up in the ceiling? And can you really picture her climbing up into an air vent and scurrying over, to drop into this room like some kind of ninja to off Mr. Dayton?"

Now that Sierra put it so succinctly, it did seem absurd. But I wasn't giving up. "That's what spies do. They look ordinary, but...." I drew my finger across my neck.

"You think she's strong enough to kill him?"

Darn it. No. No. My theory that had seemed so plausible mere seconds ago was crumbling right before my eyes.

I opened my mouth, feeling like a goldfish out of water. "Okay, this is starting to sound crazy. Still, I don't want her to leave until the police have a chance to question her."

Sierra nodded again, now all business.

Something banged against the wall from Mrs. Richardson's room.

"Right. Should we go over there and chat with her now? How long until the police are here?"

"They'll be here soon, and with a warrant."

"A warrant? Is there more evidence against her that you haven't shared yet?"

"No, it's for something Mr. Dayton stashed in the hotel vault."

Sierra nodded as she remembered. "Oh. That envelope."

"I think it's what he was killed for. So far, three people from his life have tried to pick it up."

There was a knock on the door. I squared up to the peephole to see who it was. A police hat blocked the hole.

Kristi. Relieved, I opened the door.

Immediately my mouth dropped and Sierra squealed.

It wasn't Kristi.

CHAPTER 18

The police hat's brim rose as the man slowly lifted his head. Mr. Dayton's lawyer, Austin, stared out from underneath. Austin's pupils sharpened to pinpoints at my gasp.

Anger and fear pumped through me and I shoved the door to close it. He pushed his way into the room. A second later, my brain registered his hand reaching into his jacket. He pulled out a pistol.

"Get back!" he yelled, brandishing it at us.

I let go of the door and backed up. Sierra held her hands up. Her face was pale but her eyes glowed with defiance.

That's right, girl. Stay strong.

Austin chambered a round in the gun. My mouth went dry at the metallic click. Honestly, the whole room started spinning. He directed us farther into the suite, and I moved on legs whose muscles felt like liquid.

He locked the door and then smirked at me. I realized the cap on his head wasn't a police cap, but one made to look like it, that said security. He took it off and flung it to the floor. "I heard all the commotion downstairs. Something about calling the police? Don't let a certain guest check out? I was watching. I heard your receptionist on the phone with you. I thought she wasn't at work, hmm? As soon as I saw her get in the elevator, I followed. I guess we have all the keys to the safe, now."

Adrenaline raced through me. I fought to remain calm.

"You got your key?" he asked Sierra.

She pressed her lips together and didn't respond. Grinning, he walked over to her. Sierra turned her face a few inches away as he leaned close. He reached around her neck for the flash of silver chain that peeked out from under her shirt collar. She gasped as he dug for it and slapped him.

His head froze in the direction of her slap. Slowly, he turned toward her, the gun raising as if to pistol whip her.

"Hey!" I shouted, stepping in their direction. "Austin! The

police are on their way. Just get what you want and get out of here." I swallowed, trying to conjure up spit in my mouth.

He continued to stare at Sierra. It was as if I hadn't spoken.

"Austin! Here's my key!" I pulled it off and dangled it toward him. My fingers trembled, and I balled my hand into a fist to stop it. "Take it!"

He licked his bottom lip. His eyes dragged from hers to the lanyard I held out. He leaned over and yanked it so hard the lanyard made my fingers burn. He jammed it into his pocket.

"Hands up," He faced toward me.

I raised my hands in the air. Something was odd about his beard. One corner appeared to not be lying flat.

It was fake. The slap must have disturbed the glue.

It was then that I realized where I'd recognized him from. The photo in the news article of the badge from the security officer in Milan. Austin Maricio.

"Now, back up. Get in there." Austin jerked his head toward the bathroom.

I backed up with my hands held high. My ankles felt weak.

"Go on!" he yelled.

I walked down the hallway and into the bathroom.

He turned back to Sierra. "You. Sit on the bed."

Just then we heard knocking. Hope exploded in my heart. We were rescued! A half a heartbeat later, I realized the knocking was next door.

Austin put a finger to his lips. He wrenched Sierra over by her arm and pressed the gun to her skull above her ear. "Be very quiet," he hissed. "A lot of innocent people's lives are in your hands right now."

We stood there like ice-statues, listening. I held my breath as I heard the other suite's door open, and then Mrs. Richardson's voice. The walls were too thick to make out words, but I could tell Kristi was there too.

My stomach writhed with frustration. Austin pressed the pistol harder against Sierra's head. She whimpered, and immediately any impulse to shout for help died in my throat.

Sierra tried to pull away from the end of the barrel, but he jammed against her skin again.

"Please," I whispered, begging. Cold sweat trickled down my back like spiders.

"Not a word," he hissed. He stroked the beard and his fingers found the spot that had come unglued. He pressed it back, watching me as if he dared me to say anything about it. He turned and his profile was highlighted by the window behind him, showing his nose long and sharp like it had been chiseled out of rock.

For what seemed like an eternity, we waited. My pulse thundered in my ears, blocking any sounds from next door.

Sierra's legs shook. Austin squeezed her arm, the same arm that was scarred by her abusive boyfriend, and leaned in toward her ear.

"Shhh," he whispered, almost kindly.

She shied away as though his breath smelled of putrid meat. He smiled at her reaction.

Minutes ticked by, each second holding us prisoner. I heard the suite's door shut.

My heart sank as I visualized Kristi moving away, step by step. But my crushing hopelessness was offset by Austin's removal of the gun from Sierra's head. I felt an irrational gratefulness toward him for moving it.

"Now, we wait." He gestured to the bed.

I walked back, and Sierra and I sat stiffly next to one another. He watched us for a second before pushing the pistol into the top band of his pants.

Little sounds broke the room's silence. A ticking of a clock from somewhere. Austin's deeper exhales. Soft rustles as Sierra pulled her sleeve down over her scar.

Austin paced across the living room. When his back was turned, I patted Sierra and gave her what I hoped was a strong smile. Her lips were very chapped, and she chewed on one anxiously.

"Don't worry," I whispered.

"I said, be quiet!" Austin growled from where he stood by the couch, his hand touching the butt of the pistol. He watched me for a moment, his eyes appearing flat and cold. They reminded me of the eyes in a wanted poster for a serial killer. I shivered and looked down.

He started pacing again, back and forth, back and forth. A clear path of footprints was pressed into the carpet.

I found a thread to unravel on the blanket and wound it on my finger so tightly my fingertip turned white. I did it over and over, the simple motion helping me to cope.

Time stretched out like a long rope of pizza dough. My heart cycled through periods of calming down and speeding up as panic hit me again. Sierra didn't move. She reminded me of a wounded animal whose only protection was to play dead.

Austin walked up to us. "You." He pointed to me.

Ice shot through my veins.

"Get up. Get in the bathroom." And then to Sierra, "No funny business or your boss gets it."

My legs felt disconnected to my body as I tried to command them to stand and walk. I moved toward the bathroom. As I passed down the hallway, he grabbed the back of my shirt.

"Where's your phone?"

I reached into my pocket with fingers that felt wooden and passed it over.

He glanced inside the bathroom and spied a phone on the wall.

"Go sit on the floor over there," he said, driving me toward the shower.

I moved in that direction, my hands held up, and clumsily sat on the cold tile. He ripped the receiver from the wall and then turned toward me. Not a drop of sweat or a stray hair marred his appearance. I was surprised at how in command he looked, like he did this type of thing all the time.

"You're going to stay here. This can go nice and easy or you can try to escape and get people killed. It's your choice. I'm taking her down to the safe to get what belongs to me. If you both cooperate, no one gets hurt. You do anything to cause trouble, I'll take her out, along with a few more." He stared me down. "Little lady, I suggest you do what you do best, look out for the hotel guests. You don't want a mom crying over her dead child, do you?"

My mouth went dry. I shook my head.

He left. I heard the door slam at the end of the hallway. There was a rattling noise, I assumed he was somehow tying the door so it couldn't be opened.

And then nothing.

I stood, my knees crackling from stiffness, and hurried to the end of the hall. I wanted to catch the sound of them leaving.

Taking a few slow breaths to calm my nerves, I tip-toed over and pressed my ear against the door.

Nothing. I eased my breath out slowly.

Bam!

CHAPTER 19

I reeled back from the alcove door. Frantically, I patted my body to make sure that I hadn't been shot.

"Don't test me," Austin growled from the other side. He slammed his palm against the door again. I squatted down and held myself to stop from shaking.

A moment later, the front door shut.

I squashed my face against my knees. *Think, Maisie. Think.*

There was a man armed with a gun headed to the lobby. Who knew what was about to happen, or what Sierra might resort to in a moment of panic. Nausea gnawed at my stomach at the thought of the potential disaster. I had to figure out some way to warn someone.

But how?

I headed back to the bathroom and searched the area. There was nothing. I couldn't even bang on the wall to attract attention because Mrs. Richardson was no longer there. By the time housekeeping came to clean her room or even mine, it would be too late. What was I going to do?

I covered my face in despair. Hearing my breath hit against my palms focused my attention. I breathed in, out and concentrated on the rhythm.

I can do this. There has to be away.

I hurried back out and listened again at the alcove door. When I was sure no one was in the suite, I tested the doorknob. It twisted, but the door wouldn't open. I pulled back with all my strength. My tendons and muscles screamed under the strain.

I'm not going to let this beat me!

I pictured innocent children in the foyer and braced one foot, and then the other, on the bottom of the wall beside the door and pushed with my legs as I tugged and turned. My sweaty palms nearly lost their grip, but the door didn't budge.

I stopped, panting. A feeling of hopelessness threatened to swamp me.

"No! No! No!" I yelled. My voice echoed in the alcove's hallway.

I'll figure this out. I have to.

It was then I caught sight of the closet. The ironing board! I ran into the closet and yanked the board down. I got my belly on it, and then my knee and climbed up. Carefully, I balanced the other knee up there and, with one hand sliding along the wall for balance, rose to my feet.

The board bounced under my weight. I couldn't think about that, couldn't think about anything but psyching myself up to climb into the ceiling.

I shoved the ceiling tile out of the way. Dust and drywall crumbles showered down on my face, making me spit. I grabbed the rim and tested the strength of the opening. The metal of the conduit was cool and slippery to my fingers.

This is it. I can do it.

With a grunt, I jumped up. Catching the momentum in my hands, I pushed myself as high as I could go. My legs pinwheeled under me. One foot connected with the wall. Using it to brace myself, I heaved my body into the crawlspace.

The back metal of the opening scraped against my back, making my skin burn. I squirmed and wiggled and panted, trying to get my legs through. There was nothing to grab onto. The metal sides were slick and the sweat from my fingers squeaked as I tried to keep from slipping. My weight dragged me down and I started to slide backward. Panicked, feeling like a manatee trying to squeeze through a car tire, I slowly clawed my way in.

Once inside the conduit, I lay there for a moment and tried to catch my breath. Then I army-crawled forward, following the tracks in the dust from the person before me. Had it been Austin? Or possibly someone else?

The soles of my sandals slid along the metal. I kicked them off and inched forward. I had to hurry or this would all be for nothing. There was a thin strip of light coming from the ceiling hatch in the suite next door, and I wriggled toward it. Sweat trickled down my face. It was hot in the duct, hotter than I could have ever imagined.

After thirty or so feet, I was at the next opening. The coffee pot was to one side of it, along with a cup holding a tiny brandy bottle.

I dug my fingernail around the crack of the ceiling tile. After a few tries, I was able to wedge the tile up enough to get my fingers under it. With a grunt, I slid it off and pushed it down the conduit, being careful to avoid the carafe.

Now, how to get down from here. I peered through the hole.

The only way was to lower the ironing board, which meant that once I started climbing down, I had to commit.

My imagination tried to play out a scene where I tumbled through the hole and onto the floor with broken legs, but I forced it away. I just had to do it. So, without another thought. I lowered my body through the opening.

My legs danced in the air in search of the wall that held the ironing board. Finally, I found it. I slipped my big toe into the crack—taking a moment to thank my dad for his long banana-peeling toes I'd inherited—and pulled the board down. When it was lowered enough, I climbed on it to stand.

I nearly wept with gratefulness. Instead, I jumped off the board and ran for the phone in the bathroom. I yanked it off the receiver and stared at the numbers. Horror filled me. What was Kristi's number? My heart sank as I realized I didn't remember it, having relied too long on simply pressing her name to be connected.

I hit zero.

"Oceanside Hotel, this is Clarissa speaking. How can I help you?" My sweet receptionist was so chipper, not realizing what was probably already happening in my office.

"Clarissa, this is an emergency. Sierra is on her way down, or maybe is in my office right now with a gunman. I need you to clear the lobby now and get hotel security. Do not try to stop him. Get the guests out of the way and into safety." I didn't have time for any more than that. I hung up and called 911.

When the operator answered, I told her there was a gunman with a hostage at the Oceanside hotel. The operator asked me to stay where I was and assured me help was on the way.

I sank to the cold bathroom floor, utterly deflated. I'd done all I could do. I just had to hope it was enough.

CHAPTER 20

I sat on the floor with the phone clutched to my ear. It was irrational, it wasn't like the emergency operator could keep me safe in any real way. But just hearing her calm voice made me feel like I was going to make it. Like we all were.

It felt like a lifetime, but I guess it was just a few minutes later when the operator told me the police arrived on the scene. I was surprised because I hadn't heard their sirens.

"They didn't want to alert anyone until we know how many shooters there are," she'd answered.

I nearly vomited at the word "shooters." I hadn't even considered that Austin was working with someone else. That there was a possibility of another gunman guarding the hotel's doors or skulking in the parking lot right now.

The operator told me to continue to wait there and that an officer would come get me when everything was under control.

In the end, waiting was the worst part. Much worse than facing Austin and the gun. My hands went crazy for something to do. I rubbed my neck, twisted the edge of my shirt, and paced. Endlessly paced.

Do I ignore the 911 operator and go downstairs, anyway? Will I run into Austin? Make things worse? What's going on?

I spun toward the front door of the suite at the furious pounding of footfalls in the hallway. Someone was running. I held my breath and listened. It sounded like several someones.

A second later, I heard something strike against the door. Not mine, but Mr. Dayton's.

"Maisie! We're coming in!"

It was Kristi! Quickly I flipped off the suite's locks and swung open the door. "I'm over here!" I yelled.

They'd already entered suite 360. Kristi ran back to the sound of my voice. Her mouth dropped, and she grabbed me in a hug.

"You're okay!" she gasped.

"What's happening?" I asked, desperate to know. "Are the hotel guests okay? Sierra? Did they catch him?"

"It's okay. We have him. No one got hurt." She grabbed me by the shoulders and searched my face and arms as if trying to reassure herself that I wasn't really injured. "How did you get in here? Sierra said you were tied up in the bathroom."

"I wasn't tied up, the door was tied closed somehow. I still don't know how. I used the ironing board and climbed up into the vent."

"You climbed up into the vent..." she said, glancing up.

I nodded and stood a little taller.

"I'm so proud of you!" Kristi exclaimed again. "I swear, I still remember when you were too afraid to climb in the creek to search for tadpoles. Now, look at you! Scaling walls and climbing through ceilings to save the day."

The compliment would have been better if she hadn't tagged on a memory from when I was six. Still, I smiled.

"How did you catch him?" I asked.

"We surrounded the entrance, and then I walked in. Clarissa pointed me to your office. Ryan guarded me while I kicked in the door. He gave up pretty quick with two Beretta's pointed at his face. Then Sierra gave him the coup de gras with a kick to the oysters." Kristi's lip curved. "She has a temper, that one, doesn't she?"

"You haven't seen the half of it. Good for her."

"Anyway, looky-looky," Kristi said, tapping an envelope against her palm.

"Is that the search warrant?" I asked hopefully. "Was Dayton's envelope still in there?"

"We haven't removed it yet. Finding you was my first priority after making sure Austin was taken into custody."

Movement from room 360 caught my eye. Ryan sealed the door with crime tape. I couldn't help it, seeing the door swathed in yellow made me kind of sick.

But the bad guy was in custody. I sighed and turned to go. I really needed to get downstairs and see for myself that everything was okay. Kristi walked with me as I headed to the elevator.

"You think Austin did it? Killed Dayton?" I asked as I punched the elevator button.

Kristi nodded. "He seems to have the most intel on the room. Not to mention those specific instructions to give the package to the attorney in the event of Dayton's death."

Something about her saying that bothered me, but I didn't have the time to sort it out now. The elevator door opened to reveal a very shaken Clarissa, and a defiant Sierra standing near the end of the foyer with another police officer.

I waved at Sierra, and she gave a slight smile back. For her, that was a warm reception. I could tell that she was glad to see me.

"We asked your receptionist if she felt like she needed to go to the hospital. She said no." Kristi stated.

"Just no, huh?" I asked.

Sierra turned back and glared at the officer with her arms crossed.

"I think there were a few sharper descriptives in there stating she wasn't a wimp," Kristi said wryly. She stepped back to allow me to open my office door.

I laughed, just picturing Sierra getting a chance to vent her indignation. I was glad this didn't dampen her spirit. She'd come a long way in her recovery from her past relationship.

I walked over to the safe with Kristi at my heels. Sitting on the black top was my pass-key and Sierra's as well.

It was with more than a little excitement that I grabbed mine up. "I can't believe we're finally doing this."

Kristi grabbed the other, and we stuck them in the slots and twisted.

The safe opened with a grinding clank. I swear I was holding my breath as I reached in. Slowly, I pulled the box out. My tongue dotted my bottom lip. This was it. I popped the lid, and we nearly smashed heads to look inside.

The same leather envelope rested there untouched. Kristi slid on a pair of gloves and snagged it out. She carried it to my desk.

"You ready?" She arched an eyebrow at me.

I swallowed and nodded. Of course, I was ready. I had to know if I was right.

The envelope was fastened with a string wound tightly between two toggles. She unwound it, taking what seemed like forever. I squeezed my hands and reminded myself to breathe.

Finally, it opened. She lifted the flap and peeked inside. Carefully, she upturned it and poured it out.

A velvet bag marked Cavallero.

"I was right," I whispered.

Kristi whistled. "Detective Swenson. That's what I'm going

to start calling you." She grabbed a pen from the desk and pushed apart the strings and then carefully tipped it up.

Diamonds spilled out onto an envelope on my desk. Gorgeous. Brilliant. White. The diamonds caught the overhead light and sent fiery sparkles on the paper.

"It all makes sense," I said, staring down.

"What does?"

"Like you said, Austin killed his client because he knew the jewels would go to him in the event of Dayton's death."

"But how did Austin know where Dayton was staying?" Kristi asked.

"He made the reservation for Dayton. Have you checked for Dayton's cell phone?"

"It hasn't been found yet."

"Oh." I was momentarily disturbed by the idea it was still missing, but the brilliance of the diamonds hypnotized me again.

Kristi folded the paper and poured them back into the velvet bag. "Where did you say the news said these were stolen again?"

"From the Judiciary Courthouse in Milan."

"I'll be contacting Interpol to facilitate inter-country law enforcement cooperation with the Milan police and figure out where to go next." Kristi tucked the bag back into the leather envelope and then gave my arm a squeeze. "You take care of yourself. Stay out of air vents." She huffed and shook her head. "I should jot that down on the list of things I never thought I'd have to say to you. It'll make me laugh in my old age one day."

"What was I supposed to do?" I asked. "Austin had a gun. I'm just thankful I thought of it."

A twinge hit me. There it was again. That same aggravating feeling that I was missing something.

"Well, I'm thankful you did. But one day you're going to get yourself into a situation you're not going to be able to get out yourself," Kristi admonished.

I nodded. "I know. I know. I'm trying to avoid that. But I couldn't just let him come down here without raising an alarm. I have responsibilities."

"From now on, just try to keep your responsibilities to managing the hotel and leave the detecting to us." Kristi actually shook her finger this time.

I raised a sassy eyebrow. "Hey, I suspected there'd be diamonds in there. I think I've helped a bit."

She snorted. "I knew you were going to bring that up. Fine. You've helped. But we don't need any more."

I smiled like I agreed, but deep inside I couldn't help thinking, *We'll see about that.*

"And since you've helped," she continued, "I'll give you a little reward. Forensics came back on the watch band. Surprise, surprise. It has Dayton's DNA all over it." She smirked as I groaned.

I had so hoped it had belonged to the murderer. "So it's not really a clue then," I said glumly.

"Maybe, maybe not. There was another person's DNA on it. Forensics is isolating it right now. But honestly, it could have come from anyone he came into contact with."

This time I gave her a different sort of smile. The kind that said we're about to find a killer. She might have her doubts, but I felt like we were finally on the home stretch.

CHAPTER 21

Soon after that, I left Kristi in the lobby to go find Momma. I didn't have to go far. She met me in the hallway outside our suite, one shoe on, blue paint down her cheek and splattered over a pant leg. Her fingers were stained as well. To say that Momma was freaking out would be like saying a freshly squeezed lemon was a tad tart.

"Momma? What happened?" I asked, rushing toward her.

"What happened?" Her mouth dropped. "What happened? Louisa Mae Marigold Swenson! I gave birth to you, that's what happened! And thirty-five years later, you are still scaring the crap out of me!" She whacked my arm and then squeezed me tight, her face burying into my chest. I could feel her shake as she started to cry.

"Oh, Momma!" I felt crushed and hugged her back. "I'm sorry. I didn't know you knew about everything that was going on. Honestly, I thought the police were keeping it quiet."

"I. Know. Everything," she insisted, sniffling.

I patted her. "I'm okay. Everything's okay."

After a moment, she stepped back and wiped at her tears streaming down her wrinkled cheeks, smearing the blue paint.

"Painting accident, huh?" I said, trying to lighten the mood.

She nodded and blotted under her eyes. "The kind that happens when you hear there's a gunman on the rampage and your daughter is missing."

I flushed with guilt and tried to ease her worry by saying, "Well, one bad guy down. And I can't wait to see your painting. I've heard Picasso got some of his inspiration in strange ways, too, right?"

That joke fell flatter than the narrowing glare of her eyes.

Quickly, I took the contrite route. "Got it. Sorry, Momma. It won't happen again."

"It better not. Or so help me...."

"So help you what?" I couldn't resist.

"I know where you sleep. And I have access to some pretty great craft dyes. Maybe you'd like to try fuchsia hair for a while?" She grinned back.

I raised my hands in surrender. "I'm hanging my detective hat up!"

In truth, I couldn't really and I think, deep down inside, she knew that as well. In fact, it was only a little while later that I was seated before the laptop once again.

But first, I'd sent Clarissa home. She'd been shaken and couldn't concentrate. Sierra had said she was fine, but when she saw Clarissa get time off, she decided she needed a break too. All the rest of the staff was abuzz with what happened, and gossip was running strange. Luckily, the guests had been oblivious to all the drama.

I did my best to wrangle everyone back into focusing on their jobs. Then I went to my office and had my own private break down. After a few tears, and three paperclips straightened, I turned my attention to the computer.

Austin was in custody, and that should have made me happy. But something about the whole thing bothered me.

Why did he lock me in the bathroom alcove? Shouldn't he have thought about the possibility that I could escape from the room the same way he got in? After all, the ironing board was still down.

It was such a small detail that I kept pushing it away. He probably had other things on his mind, like a kidnapping and all. Maybe he assumed I didn't know about the connecting duct.

But as hard as I tried, I just couldn't buy that excuse. Working the last few years with the public taught me a bit about human nature. And one thing I learned was that humans often glance at the thing they want to avoid. But he hadn't acted like the thought had occurred to him at all.

I searched up the original news article and skimmed it again.

Judge reprimands courthouse security.

Judge Corroley called out courthouse security, Austin Maricio for failing to guard evidence gathered against one of the mob bosses, Dario Torino. The diamonds, estimated in the millions, disappeared overnight. Judge Corroley was forced to drop charges against Mr. Torino in light of the missing evidence. Torino was accused of having a long reaching arm clear to NY with affiliations with third circuit judge Martin Davis.

Maricio has since disappeared. He was last seen at the courthouse with an unidentified man in his late fifties. Images from courthouse cameras give us this picture.

I studied the picture. I could clearly identify Maricio as Austin now, both by his nose and his clean-shave, now knowing he wore a fake beard. I studied the back of the second man. I bet it was Dayton, and those dark pants were the black pants rolled in Dayton's suitcase.

I leaned back in the chair, paper clip twirling in my fingers, and made a mental list of my questions. What was Dayton's involvement in this? How did he get the diamonds? And where was his cell phone? I didn't believe he didn't have one, especially being an international traveler.

I did know that Dayton had used the hotel phone several times. I clicked a few links until the hotel's room phone records came up, and then scanned his out-going and in-coming records. There weren't many, and they were all to the front desk or from me.

Except for two numbers. A quick internet search of the area codes showed one was for Connecticut, and one was for New Jersey. Both calls were made sometime after he'd first checked in. I hesitated and then rang up the New Jersey number.

"Highwater Hotel. How can I help you?"

"Hi there. Where exactly are you located again?" I asked.

"We're about two miles from the airport, in Lexington, New Jersey," the receptionist answered back.

I thanked her and hung up. He called a hotel in New Jersey, huh? I took a second to study the second number. Well, here goes nothing. I dialed it up.

It rang.

And rang.

There was no answering machine. I was just about to hang up when I heard, "Hello?"

It was a woman with a soft voice. She sounded vaguely familiar. I was so surprised, it took me a second to answer back.

"H-hi. I think I have the wrong number," I stammered.

"Wrong number? Ms. Swenson, is this you?"

I nearly dropped the phone at the mention of my name. "Yes?"

"It's me, Julie. I heard a phone ringing and went to answer it."

"You did? Where are you?"

"Mrs. Richardson's room."

I'd forgotten all about Mrs. Richardson and the fact that her room was being flipped for a new guest.

"The phone was in the closet." Julie's voice lifted in a question at the last word. I knew she was thinking about the duct between this room and Dayton's.

"Was the ironing board up or down?"

"It was up. The phone was under a pile of wet towels in the corner. I would have scooped it up with the laundry if it hadn't started to ring."

"I'm coming up to the room. Don't touch it."

She hesitated. "Ms. Swenson, I'm talking on it."

I groaned. "Just hang up and set it down. I'm on my way."

I traveled the elevator to what was starting to feel like a well-beaten path to the thirty-first floor. Suite 359's door was blocked open with a cart in the entryway. I squeezed past it and into the room.

"Julie?" I called.

"Right here, boss."

I grabbed a pair of gloves from the cart and pulled them on. Julie stood at the alcove entry with a phone between her two white shoes. Her cheeks flushed when she saw me.

"I put it right down when you said to."

I tried not to laugh at how literal she took it. Hands gloved, I bent down and clicked the phone on. *Okay, little phone. Give me your secrets. Where did you come from and who do you belong to?*

It required a password, making me sigh.

"No, don't worry," Julie said. "Just hold it up to the light."

I looked at her questioning. Were we all so tired now that none of us were making sense anymore? "The light?"

"Yeah. Look for fingerprints or a squiggle."

I did as she said and found four imprints on the keypad over the two, three, seven and nine. "Yeah, there's four."

"Four marks, that's great. It means there's no repetition."

I nodded like I knew what she was talking about. I had no idea.

Julie recognized I was bluffing. "That's good news. No repeats means it will only take twenty-four chances to get it right."

"Have you done this before?" Suddenly, Julie wasn't looking so innocent.

"Hey, I know things. I've got brothers." She shrugged.

I took a deep breath and pressed a key. Nothing happened. My finger didn't make the screen pad react.

"You should cut the fingertip off of it." Julie teased.

My mouth dropped open.

Julie's expression changed to surprise. "What? I was just kidding."

"No. Julie! I just remembered a glove tip that Mike found that first night. It wasn't from us. It was from whoever crawled through!" I patted my jacket, disgusting I know, but I found it. It rolled in my palm.

She stared at like it was a rare beetle, slightly repulsed and slightly fascinated. "You think it has a fingerprint?"

"Maybe?" I ran to the bathroom and ripped off a piece of toilet paper. Carefully, I rolled it up to save for Kristi.

"Now, seriously, is there a trick to get the screen to read my touch?" I asked.

"Breath on your finger."

"Hmm?"

"Warm the glove tip with your breath. It moistens it and makes the screen think it's your skin."

I tried it and it worked. I flashed her a smile and started the combinations.

Sixteen attempts was the magical number. On that last try, the screen unlocked and opened up to the main screen. Was it Mrs. Richardson's? Was it Austin's? Julie and I leaned over to read it.

Games. Lots of games. Not exactly what I thought I'd find on Mrs. Richardson's phone. I went into settings and checked the account. Everything was blank. I scrolled to contacts. Nothing.

It proved to me that this had to be a burner phone. But whose was it?

I went to recent numbers called. There was only one. "I'm doing it," I said a little forcefully.

"For sure." She cleared her throat. "After all. We need to figure out who's phone this is."

I pressed dial. It rang once. Twice.

"Hello? D. R. Austin, attorney at law's office"

I hung up the phone, my face heating from the rush of blood. "It was him! This phone belongs to the lawyer who murdered Dayton."

Julie looked confused. "He kidnapped Sierra. Obviously, it was him."

"No." I shook my head. "It wasn't obvious. I knew he knew about the envelope, but I wasn't positive it was him who crawled through the ductwork. He must have done it earlier that day and waited for the right moment to pounce on Dayton. Then he climbed back through to this and dropped his phone, making his escape." I clutched the rubber glove tip still wrapped in the toilet paper. "This might really cinch it. Maybe there's a fingerprint in the glove."

207

Julie twisted her mouth in skepticism. "You've been watching too many mystery shows. These gloves are filled with a powder. You aren't going to get a print from them."

I scowled. "You never know. Forensic science is amazing these days."

She sniffed. "When my uncle Oliver had his car stolen, the police couldn't do anything about it. We even had footage from the store."

"Well, I'm sorry about that. But I have hope."

She clucked her tongue and grabbed her glass cleaner. "If there's nothing else...?"

I shook my head. "No. Nothing else. I'll get these to Kristi. Call me if you happen to find another clue."

She spun around, sassy. "I will, although I'll be making sure it won't end up forgotten in my pocket."

Smart-aleck.

CHAPTER 22

I didn't have a chance to forget the glove piece in my pocket again because Kristi came by right away to collect it. She seemed to think the same as Julie that it was a long shot, but she carefully bagged it all the same. She was much more excited about the cell phone.

"What happened with Mrs. Richardson?" I asked. "Is she a suspect any more?"

"She wasn't ever really a suspect. We considered her a person of interest. We talked with her when Austin held you captive, and, as unpleasant as she is, her story checked out. But we're still keeping her on the radar."

I nodded. "And the watch strap? Anything more about that?"

"Nothing yet. With Dayton's DNA on it, I can't say they're

looking too hard. Like I told you earlier, he could have picked up the other person's DNA at any time." Kristi eyed me and touched my arm. "Listen. You look worn out. Is there any way you can take the afternoon off? Maybe just get some rest? Stress has a way of catching up once things calm down. We've got our man. You don't have to worry anymore."

She was right. I needed to get off the hamster wheel of spinning these so-called clues my brain picked up and tried to figure out. I agreed, and we made plans to have a girl's night soon, along with Ruby.

I checked in with the front desk. Everything seemed to be ticking away as usual. I headed for my office with a cup of coffee and a protein bar from the vending machine. I'd actually picked a candy bar, but the machine spit out the protein snack instead, and I took it as a sign that I better pump up the effort to eat healthier.

I peeled back the wrapper and turned on the computer screen. While it was booting, I took a bite. Dry, chalkiness filled my mouth. What the heck was I eating? I chucked it into the trash before washing my mouth out with a sip of coffee.

My mind went back to that brandy and the cigar. Camacho. Was it a special brand? Did it come from Madrid or Milan? I typed in the name and hit enter.

It turned out it came from neither, but rather from Connecticut. I bit my lip, thinking. The cigar was famous for the same state where Mr. Austin, Dayton's attorney was from. Was that just a coincidence?

The line from Momma's crime TV channel came back to me from a few days ago. "There's no such thing as a coincidence when it comes to murder." Just like the calories from the cake I'd been eating, that phrase had stuck with me.

I typed in D.R. Austin's name in the search bar. Not surprisingly, his law firm was the first link to come up. I clicked the link.

The page loaded with the usual fanfare of lawyerese speech about how he was the only one who could save the potential client from whatever it was they were facing. I scrolled for a picture on the page.

Wait a minute. What was this? My spine stiffened, and I leaned forward.

There was no picture. But there was a name. Devin Richardson Austin.

I swallowed as a chill pricked at the hairs on the back of my neck. How could I have been so wrong? But it turned out that I'd been right too! When would I learn to trust my gut feeling?

I typed in the name in a search engine to double check and scanned through the images that came up.

Bingo. I hit the winning load. It was of an awards ceremony. The headline stated, "Devin Richardson Austin wins an unprecedented case against impeachment." My jaw dropped. It was Mrs. Richardson who was Dayton's lawyer, not David Austin.

Another search turned up a marathon. Mrs. Richardson was staring straight ahead and ignoring the camera. But her sharp nose on her determined face was unmistakable. But what was that on her wrist? I zoomed in.

It was the same watch band I'd found on the floor. I zoomed in farther and gasped. The fastener was on the same hole as what was marked on the band. Number four.

I swallowed hard while my finger searched for a paperclip. It *had* been Mrs. Richardson who been the person in Dayton's room.

Which meant one thing.

She was the killer.

I typed the only person I knew who could help.—**Kristi, I need to talk to you ASAP**

She texted back. —**What's up?**

—No, I need a phone call. I chewed my thumbnail impatiently.

—I can do it in about an hour.

An hour? Was I going to have to wait that long? Frustrated, I saved the picture of Mrs. Richardson at the marathon and then sent it to Kristi. Then I cropped Mrs. Richardson's wrist and forwarded that as well.

My phone rang immediately.

"Maisie, what are you playing at?" Kristi whispered.

"Why are you whispering? Are you busy?"

"Yes, hence, the 'I'll call you back in an hour' text." Graham crackers couldn't be drier than the tone she used.

Time was limited. I rushed out my words. "I searched up Mr. Austin's law agency and found the name D. R. Austin. Guess what? He was masquerading as Dayton's lawyer, not realizing the lawyer really was a woman. In fact, it was Mrs. Richardson. The picture I just sent you was taken last year. You can see the watch on her wrist. And when I zoomed in, I could see it was tightened to the fourth notch, just like the band we found."

Kristi was silent. I continued to try to convince her. "Don't you see? She set this whole thing up. She reserved the room for Dayton and even the one next to it."

"There's a lot of information you're giving me here. Answer me this. Why didn't she take the suite the first time she reserved it? And how did Richardson know that you'd assign it to her later?"

"She worded her complaints very specifically. She's well traveled, it must have been a calculated risk she was willing to take." I thought for a second, my finger untwisting a paperclip.

"A risk, huh?" Kristi didn't sound like she was buying it.

Her skepticism was contagious. "Give me a second. I'll call you right back," I said in a rush. There was one thing left I still hadn't checked.

Dayton had said something that first night when I'd asked him if he wanted me to call his lawyer for some support. His face had drained of blood and he'd mumbled something about how everyone betrayed him.

My fingers flew across the keys and I pulled up his room's phone records again. I saw the call to his attorney's burner phone and, right after that, was his phone call to the hotel in New Jersey.

Something from his conversation with his lawyer must have spurred that hotel call.

Following my hunch, I called the hotel again.

On the third ring, it was answered. "Highwater hotel, this is Marjorie speaking. How can I help you?"

"Hi, Marjorie. This is Maisie Swenson, General Manager at the Oceanside in Starke Springs, Florida. One of our guests called there to make a reservation. Would you be able to check on that?" I bluffed a little on my reason.

"Absolutely." Her voice brimmed with confidence. "What's his name?"

Here it was. The defining moment. "Vincent Dayton."

Fast typing that sounded like a box of dice being shaken came through the phone's speaker. After a moment, she said, "Yes... it appears he did have a reservation, but it was for two days ago. He never showed up. Would you like me to reschedule it?"

"Not at this time but I'll let you know." I hung up. I was having a hard time wrapping my mind around the fact that Mrs. Richardson really was Devin Richardson Austin, his attorney. But there was no denying that something in that conversation seemed to spur Dayton to try to leave our hotel early than her original reservation of a few days.

So, what had happened during that phone call? Whatever it was, it must have been dramatic since Richardson didn't show up for her official reservation, either. Instead, she'd disguised herself as a random guest and complained about needing a room with a better view.

And then there was that letter that I'd found in between the sheets of the bible. It had read... in the event of my death, give my belongings to my... and the word had cut off.

I'd assumed he'd been about to write the word, "attorney." But he'd already left instructions like that. Why write them again?

Something must have happened to make him not trust her, and the letter was for a new name.

I searched up Devin Richardson. An article popped up about a blurb in a local newspaper for her wedding day. It was simple: Gerald Richardson and Devin Austin married on the 24th of October in Scottsdale Connecticut. That explained her two last names. It was odd she used Richardson before the Austin. It made me wonder if she legally changed it that way so she could use her maiden name as an attorney.

I searched for her maiden name, Devin Austin. A grainy black-and-white picture showed up of a very young-looking Devin Austin (AKA Mrs. Richardson) standing next to a boy in his late teens. She wore a tutu and leotard and stood on point while the teen boy seemed to ignore her. Underneath the picture it said, *Ballerina Devin Austin gives brother, David, a few pointers.*

In the picture, I glimpsed a tiny fraction of the adult version of her in the intensity of her stare. The photo almost made me feel sorry for her. She had a wistful expression, lower lip slightly open, eyes locked on the camera. Almost as if she were waiting for approval from whoever was behind the lens. I remembered how her voice had dipped the day we'd met in the hall. I'd commented on the ribbon in her hair and she said she had to give up Juilliard for a new career. My guess was that the career her parents pushed her into was law.

Her brother gazed out into the distance as if someone had just called his name. I recognized him right away as Austin, the man who'd told us he was Dayton's lawyer. His nose had the same distinct sharpness as his sister's. Their parents had used the same letter for both of their first names, so it hadn't been hard for him to impersonate her as a lawyer.

After pushing the keyboard forward, I grabbed out a pad of paper and drew a chart to make it clear. Devin Richardson Austin was Dayton's lawyer. Her brother was David Austin, who impersonated her to get the envelope Dayton left in our hotel safe. Together, the brother and sister had run a scam to use Dayton as a mule and then steal the diamonds. Now I just needed to track down who the uncle was who called. And who was Stephenson?

CHAPTER 23

I typed the words, "Vincent Dayton's brother" into the search engine. I just wanted to check. I realized that the one main reason why I didn't believe Stephenson was Dayton's half-brother was because of something Austin had said. And, obviously, Austin hadn't proved himself too trustworthy.

I scrolled through the pictures. Most were of athletes or other people with the same name. But one caught my attention. It was of the short man leaving a restaurant, and even better, a few steps behind him was Vincent Dayton. Even in the picture, Vincent looked anxious, brushing his hair back. I clicked it to read an article from the NY Times. *Local legend, Vito Stephenson, leaves the family restaurant with his brother.*

Hmm. So it *was* true that Vincent Dayton was half-siblings with a Vito Stephenson.

My cell rang. Kristi.

"I don't have all the answers yet," I said, to head off what I expected Kristi to ask. Then, I filled her in about how Vincent made a phone call to a different hotel to make a reservation after his talk with his attorney, and that Vincent and Vito Stephenson appeared to be half-brothers after all.

"Well, I have news for you too," Kristi said. "So the Milan Polizia just got back to us. From their investigation transcripts, mob boss, Dario Torino, was apprehended leaving the Cavallero jewelry store after giving it an apparent shakedown. Dario was discovered concealing the bag of diamonds on him."

She took a deep breath and continued in her machine gun style. "During Dario's trial, Austin, who went by the name Austin Maricio and worked as a security guard, decided to steal them. Austin talked with his sister, Devin Richardson, who in turn talked with Dayton, her client. She convinced Dayton into flying out to Milan to be used as a mule to bring the diamonds home. And she gave him the disclaimer letter that his belongings would go to her in the event of his death."

Excitement made me smile. The bag inside the leather

envelope had said Cavallero on it, so the pieces of evidence were finally making some sense.

I grabbed a rubber band and slid it over my wrist and started to spin it. "I'm pretty sure Dayton was supposed to meet Mrs. Richardson here at the hotel to drop off the diamonds. But something happened during their last phone call that made him change his mind. I think he told her not to show up, or he'd run, which is why she didn't check in on the day she was supposed to. Instead, she came the next day, disguised as a pushy, complaining guest."

"So it was just pure luck that she got the room next door?" Kristi asked.

I stretched the band, thinking. "Not luck, exactly. She probably knew what things to say to get that upgrade, and she knew the room was still vacant, waiting for her original reservation. Maybe she overheard one of the staff mention there was a critic coming and knew she had some leverage. But she gambled for it, and it worked out for her." I got up and started to pace the tiny room. "Maybe she originally meant to just search his suite for the diamonds when he was gone. But he was too paranoid to leave. I'm guessing she staged the brandy and glass to continue to freak him out."

Kristi made a noise of agreement.

"And he started a new letter that I found in his bible. I

thought the word that had been interrupted meant A for attorney, but maybe it was for another name. Richardson knew he didn't trust her so she killed him. But how did she do it?" I asked.

"I'm not sure yet. I'm guessing some type of poison at the moment, something that she mixed with the alcohol to provide a fatal effect. What she didn't expect was that he would vomit up the mixture. From the blood settling pattern, our theory is that he died in the bathroom. Somehow, she dragged him back to the bed where she posed him."

It sounded like Kristi took a sip of something before she continued. "It was about that time when Mike, your security guy, knocked on the door. She opened it to the safety chain, being careful to stay out of sight, and used a hoarse whisper to answer Mike's questions. Then it was just a matter of wiping everything down to get rid of fingerprints, clipping his nails, and removing the cup and brandy bottle she'd staged the night before. Richardson then climbed back through the vent and, after leaving everything in the conduit, went back to her room."

I nodded, even though Kristi couldn't see me. "She was so good. She even complained about the noise upstairs. I remember her door had been open, and she must have heard Dayton tell us about it that night when we were leaving. She wanted to give herself an alibi too. Because what Dayton had heard wasn't from the room above, but actually her crawling through the vent."

"That makes sense," Kristi nodded. "And she probably lost her burner phone when she climbed back into her room during one of those trips. You gave her more trouble when you wouldn't release the belongings to her brother, who was impersonating her."

"So he got desperate and tried to force us to open the safe." I mused, feeling a bit overwhelmed at the memory. "They almost got away with it."

Kristi clucked her tongue in a no-nonsense way. "Not with you on the case."

I grinned. It was nice to be appreciated even if I did bungle things up more often than I figured them out.

CHAPTER 24

a week had gone by, and I felt as run down as a pair of sneakers after a marathon. The murder was solved, with no following fanfare, no news story, and no picture in the newspaper for helping to catch the Milan jewel thieves. The Milan police extradited Austin, the courthouse security guard, along with his sister Devin Richardson, to Italy where they awaited their trial.

The PR team for Oceanside hotel did their best to squelch any connection to the jewel thieves. Poor (or not so poor, depending on how one viewed a mule for stolen property) Mr. Dayton's death didn't even get so much as a blurb in our local paper.

I couldn't help thinking *poor*. He'd been so frightened and convinced he'd been haunted by ghosts. I still remember how desperately he'd gripped my arm while staring at me with beseeching eyes to believe him.

My heart felt heavy as I applied my mascara. I was finally getting my date with Jake, one that was long past due. He'd flown in last night from his business trip and I missed him so much. It was amazing how quickly one started to rely on another person for support, and I'd gone through a lot these last few days without him.

My phone rang, and I picked it up, expecting it to be him. It was Kristi.

"So we got the forensics report, and I thought you'd like to know." Kristi began without even saying hi. "The lab found traces of Benzodiazepines in the coffee pot, along with the dregs in one of the wine bottles. Devin Richardson hasn't admitted to any of this, but we surmise that during her first visit, when she posed the brandy bottle, she grabbed Dayton's sleeping pills. Back in her room, she pounded the pills into dust and dissolved them completely in water in her coffee pot. Then she crawled back over and poured the liquid into the opened wine bottle. My guess is that she removed the drinking glasses, so he was forced to drink from the bottle, which further hid the tampering. As for the DNA on the watch strap, they're still investigating that. But they've isolated that it came from a woman. I suspect it'll turn out to be Richardson's, and Dayton's actually got on it when she dragged the body from the bathroom. Finally, as far as who the uncle was who spoke with you on the phone, we're at a loss. But with our suspects in custody, it's a moot point. And with that, I get to say my favorite phrase. Case closed."

"Wow. The cause of death was the last piece of the puzzle for me. I remember your partner finding the near-empty bottle."

"She probably left a few to make it look less suspicious. Anyway, I hope this news helps you relax now."

"I'll try. Thanks for calling, Kristi."

"Anytime. And the next time we talk, let's just focus on some good ol' local gossip. I know Ruby has a few stories. She feels neglected, you know."

"Lunch next week," I promised and we hung up.

About a half-hour later, just as I was slipping on my shoes, I heard Bingo baying. *Jake must be here.* I thanked God for that dog because Momma wouldn't have let me know Jake was here until she'd had a good long conversation with him, probably including a perusal through my baby photo album.

The thought of it sent shivers down my spine and I ran out of my room.

Momma had indeed let him in and now stood with her hand hooked over his arm.

"Maisie!" she exclaimed. "Look who showed up."

"I've got it from here, Momma," I said, shooing her away. She left, but not without a little harrumph.

"Hi," Jake's smile was as smooth as his voice. His eyes moved to take me in. "Love. The dress."

"This old thing?" I said, giving a little twirl. I'd seen it half-price at the Dress Expo and grabbed it up. Blue and curve-hugging, I knew the best part of the dress was from behind, and I could tell by his sudden intake of breath that he thought so too. I'd been working on that booty, so I was feeling pretty confident.

"Hmm, maybe take another spin so I can make sure," he said.

I laughed and pushed his arm. "Where are we going?"

He grinned. "I was thinking maybe the Steak Grill?"

"That sounds wonderful!" I looped my arm through his and walked with him to his car.

"So, I have something to show you," Jake said after I'd gotten in. He reached behind the seat and tossed something on my lap. It was a page from a newspaper, carefully folded into a square.

"What's this?" I asked, picking it up.

"Read it," he advised, his eyes in the rearview mirror.

Carefully, he backed the car out of the stall.

I opened it up. Bold letters screamed out at me. **Oceanside Hotel surfs the high seas in my books!**

What?

I flicked my gaze over to him curiously.

"Keep going," he advised. He flipped on his blinker and pulled out onto the road. I was kept from reading more as he gunned it, jerking me back into the seat. The corner of his lip quirked.

"Show off," I teased.

"What?" he said, speeding up even more.

I shook my head and read out loud. "The Oceanside hotel boasts of its five-star rating, and it's easy to see why. From the gorgeous rooms, attentive staff, food service, and the attention to details, you'll never want to leave this hotel."

My grin kept me from reading more. "Aww! How is this possible?"

Jake raised an eyebrow. "Your name is in there. I made sure to let my brother know."

I glanced back at the article. "General Manager Maisie Swenson is as personable as she is professional. Despite her busy schedule, she took the time to meet with individual guests and see that their needs were provided for. I have her personally to thank for my lack of a sunburn."

My mouth dropped open in bewilderment. Was it really her? I scanned for the writer's name. Jennifer Parkins.

Seriously? The woman who'd been the complete antithesis of what a hotel reviewer normally appeared? Happy. Content. Appreciative? She was the critic?

I tipped my head and laughed. Just when I thought I understood human nature, someone flipped the chart again.

"What's so funny?" Jake asked. "I thought you'd like it."

"I do. I do. It's just that I thought I'd been so smart to figure out who the reviewer was so I could cater to her every need. She probably was shocked to see me all the time."

"Who's she?"

"Mrs. Richardson. The murderer." I answered. My fingers went to my wrist and then fell away at the lack of a rubber band.

Jake seemed to notice the gesture. He flipped on his blinker.

"Where are we going? This isn't the way to the Steak Grill." I set the paper next to me and sat straighter in the seat.

"You have been so busy, I thought it'd be nice to really get away."

Anticipation fluttered in my stomach. "What did you do?"

"Don't get too excited. It's just a small thing," he warned. He pulled into the Starke Springs city park and found a spot for the car. I could tell he was excited by the zip in his step as he jumped out. He hurried around while I watched in wonder, and then he opened my door.

"You ready?" he asked, offering his hand.

I took it and allowed him to help me from the low seat. I never did feel very graceful trying to maneuver out of a car in a tight skirt and heels, but the smile he gave me made me feel like a princess.

"What are you up to?" I asked again before leaning down to look for my purse. I scooped it up and turned back.

"It's been four months since we got together, you know," he said, grabbing my hand into his.

"You keeping track?" I asked teasingly.

He shut the door and locked it, then gave me a smile. "Come on."

Hand in hand, he led me down to the paved path. I tried to coax the destination out from him again, but he just lifted his eyebrow and gave a casual shrug.

"Tell me!" I insisted.

"So impatient," he said as we rounded a group of trees.

The park was empty at this time of night, but it wasn't quiet. In fact, now that I was concentrating on it, I could hear music. Violins.

I chuckled and briefly closed my eyes. He still didn't say anything as we walked along the gently winding trail.

The sun had nearly set, and the surroundings were softly grayed. I lifted my head to search as the music grew louder.

Up ahead was the park's white gazebo. It glowed from what appeared to be hundreds of tiny white lights. A table, decked with a white tablecloth, stood in the center.

"Join me for dinner?" Jake whispered in my ear. His warm breath sent shivers down my spine.

I nodded instead of speaking and he led me to the gazebo steps. To one side sat four violinists. The hauntingly beautiful music swelled around us as Jake pulled out one of the chairs.

"I can't believe you did this," I murmured, trying to take it all in.

"It's been four months. I wanted to celebrate."

I smiled gratefully at him. My heart sang at being with someone who appreciated spending time with me that I felt the same way about.

The table held a vase of white roses, which he moved to one side. He reached for my hand again. "How do you feel about peanut-butter-and-jelly sandwiches?"

A snicker shot out of me. "Only if it's grape jelly."

"Grape jelly? I didn't realize you were so picky. We might be in trouble then because all I have is strawberry."

A waitress seemed to materialize out of nowhere holding a bottle of wine. Jake took it from her and poured two small amounts for us to sample. He was a sommelier and knew his stuff.

"Red wine pairs with peanut butter. I never knew," I joked.

He swirled his glass and breathed in. "This is Sangiovese. Which perfectly pairs with filet mignon." His eyes twinkled. "I did promise you a steak."

I made an appreciative noise and tried to imitate his sniff of the wine. He sent the glass down and pulled out a thin box from his jacket pocket.

"For you," he said. "In celebration."

I took the gift box, feeling a bit unsure. What could he be giving me? It had only been four months. With a quick glance to him—and noting his pleased expression— I slid off the ribbon and slowly opened the box.

Inside, lay a black leather cord. A few tiny silver and enameled blue beads were strung along it.

"It's for your wrist," he explained, nodding to my arm. "You know how you usually keep a rubber band there? I thought this might work instead."

Heat flushed my cheeks at his thoughtful gesture. The fact that he knew my tick and didn't judge me, but actually cared, touched my heart so deeply I felt tears prickle my eyes.

"Here, let me see." He took the box from me and carefully removed the bracelet. Then he reached for my arm. The bracelet tickled as he slid it around my wrist. It took him a few seconds as his big fingers struggled with the silver clasp, but finally, he fastened it.

I looked at it under the sparkling lights. "It's beautiful," I whispered.

He cupped my chin, his thumb softly stroking my cheek. His eyes stared deep into mine. "It's strong, beautiful, and one-of-a-kind. Just like you are."

I ran my fingers over the bracelet with a happy sigh, not quite believing how lucky I was. Life was such a crazy, wonderful, amazing, frustrating, exhilarating adventure. There definitely were some rollercoaster lows, but boy, were they worth the peaks that followed.

The Honeyed Taste of Deception

The Tempting Taste of Danger

The Frosty Taste of Scandal

Made in the USA
San Bernardino, CA
23 December 2019